IGUANA BOY

VS. THE 30 SECOND THIEF!

HODDER CHILDREN'S BOOKS
FIRST PUBLISHED IN GREAT BRITAIN IN 2018 BY HODDER AND STOUGHTON
1 3 5 7 9 10 8 6 4 2

A CIP CATALOGUE RECORD FOR THIS BOOK
IS AVAILABLE FROM THE BRITISH LIBRARY.

ISBN 978 1 444 93940 8

PRINTED AND BOUND IN GREAT BRITAIN BY
CLAYS LTD, ELCOGRAF S.P.A

THE PAPER AND BOARD USED IN THIS BOOK
ARE MADE FROM WOOD FROM RESPONSIBLE SOURCES.

HODDER CHILDREN'S BOOKS
AN IMPRINT OF
HACHETTE CHILDREN'S GROUP
PART OF HODDER AND STOUGHTON
CARMELITE HOUSE
50 VICTORIA EMBANKMENT
LONDON EC4Y 0DZ

AN HACHETTE UK COMPANY
WWW.HACHETTE.CO.UK

WWW.HACHETTECHILDRENS.CO.UK

CONTENTS

Dylan

Paul

Crazy
Red-Eye
Paul

Pauline

Smelly
Paul

Arctic Thunder
Millie Monday
Terrifying Suzanne
Atomic Adam
A
Ron Strongman

¡Hola!
Hugo

COUNTDOWN TO HQ

Have you ever had a dream that felt so real, you couldn't tell if you were awake or asleep? The kind of dream where you stop to pinch yourself, but you *still* don't wake up? If you were to wake up, you might even look down and see a red mark where you pinched your skin a little too hard. Then a unicorn flies past riding on the back of a vacuum cleaner and says hello to you in Spanish – 'HOLA!' – and it becomes pretty obvious that you ARE asleep.

That's EXACTLY how Dylan Spencer was feeling about becoming a superhero. It felt like a dream, but it wasn't – there were no Spanish-speaking unicorns in sight, Dylan REALLY WAS a superhero and he was *definitely* wide awake.

Dylan Spencer, in his short reign as an awesome superhero, had defeated the Platypus Kid, a supervillain hell-bent on world domination, and saved every superhero, and consequently THE ENTIRE WORLD. He couldn't have achieved any of this without the help of his best friends Paul, Crazy Red-Eye Paul, Smelly Paul and Pauline – who all happened to be iguanas.

Yes, Dylan was IGUANA BOY and his superpower was talking to iguanas. Without them, he would be nothing.

His prize for **SAVING THE WORLD** was to be welcomed into the Superhero Collective, the neatest organisation ever, which aimed to bring all superheroes together for one common goal: to use their superpowers for the benefit of mankind.

★

Dylan's first day as a fully fledged superhero was only a few hours away and, unsurprisingly, he was having trouble getting to sleep. His palms were sweaty and his stomach kept doing somersaults, as he thought of all the cool missions he would get to go on. He closed his eyes, determined to get some sleep.

'And then I was all like, K'POW!' said Crazy Red-Eye Paul, suddenly, flinging himself off the bookshelf above Dylan's bed, his back legs stretched out in front of him. He landed in a heap on Dylan's pillow, slapping him square in the face with his scaly tail.

'Please, Red-Eye, I have to get some sleep, it's the biggest day of my life tomorrow,' said Dylan, rolling over to face the wall.

'Don't you mean *second* biggest? Remember that time we saved the WORLD from the evil Platypus Kid? I certainly do, I was all like, K'POW! And then I did like a really cool cartwheel followed by a kind of SKA'PLUNK!' Red-Eye sprang into the air, landing on Dylan's back before performing a pathetic karate chop on his shoulders.

'Please be quiet,' said Paul, poking his scaly head out of the cage. Dylan could see that the other iguanas had buried their heads in a pile of bark, but it didn't look like it was helping any of them get to sleep.

Their tails were twitching.

'Just ignore him,' said Pauline, who had climbed out of the cage and was now resting on the pillow beside Dylan. The other three iguanas also gathered around him.

'I can't believe we are going to the real-life Superhero HQ tomorrow! Is it true that the building floats high up over the river in London?' asked Smelly Paul.

'It really does,' said Dylan, admitting defeat and sitting up to reach under his bed and pull out a dusty poster. As he unrolled it, the iguanas gasped. Beautifully illuminated by the sunny skyline, a clear glass building hovered above the water.

'How on earth will we get up there? Will

your brother and sister show us the way?' asked Pauline.

'Yep, Sam and Millie will take us. Apparently, Ron Strongman himself asked them to bring us.'

'Wow. That. Is. AMAZING! But seriously,

who is Don Stronghands?' asked Crazy Red-Eye Paul. 'His name sounds familiar.'

'It's *Ron Strongman* – the head of the Superhero Collective. The *most* important guy on the planet. He's the one we will need to impress if we're ever going to make it as supercool superheroes,' Dylan replied, sighing wistfully.

'I'm sure we will. Remember that time— '

'SHUT UP!' the iguanas shouted in unison, before Red-Eye could even finish his thought. Paul clipped him around the back of his head with his tail.

'What? I wasn't going to say what you think I was going to say,' said Red-Eye rubbing the back of his head delicately.

'Go on, Red-Eye, what were you going to say?' Dylan picked him up and gently moved him onto his chest.

'I was going to say, before I was RUDELY interrupted ... do you remember that time ... when ... we were all here ... in this very room ... talking about ... how I SINGLE-HANDEDLY DEFEATED THE PLATYPUS KID WITH A GIANT KABLAMO!'

Dylan threw Red-Eye, launching him across the room and into the cage.

'That's enough, Paul, it's time to get some sleep,' he said. 'I need to be up in time to shower and decide what I'm going to wear. First impressions will be key. I want to look and smell good, so Ron Strongman notices me for the right reasons. No offence Smelly Paul,' he added, patting the iguana on the head.

Smelly Paul raised his arms to show there were no hard feelings, catching a whiff of his own armpit in the process. If they could bottle that smell, Dylan could grow an empire selling the best stink bomb in the world.

7:58AM

Dylan looked at his clock. It was 7.58 a.m. His brother and sister had been very clear that they were leaving the house with or without him at precisely 8 a.m. Dylan noticed that Pauline's tail was draped over the alarm clock. *Great*, Dylan thought to himself, *she must have hit the off button in her sleep.*

Dylan jumped to his feet so quickly that he stumbled forward off the other end of the bed, landing in a heap on an old pizza box.

The thud woke the iguanas, who looked up to see a panic-ridden Dylan wearing a large dollop of cheese on his forehead from landing on a slice of triple-cheese pizza.

The sound of sniggering could be heard coming from downstairs. He should have known. His brother and sister were overjoyed that he might miss his first day at Superhero HQ and sabotage his one chance of being a superhero.

'I guess he must have overslept,' he heard his brother say snidely. 'Never mind, Millie, I'm sure Ron will realise his mistake. I mean, Dylan's superpower is talking to iguanas. Hardly going to save the world again, is he?'

Dylan ignored them and slipped his right foot into an old sock he found on the floor, and pulled a T-shirt over his head – one that had been hanging over his bedroom door to dry. He stepped his left foot forward into another sock whilst pulling on a pair of trousers from the wash basket. Tugging at the waistband, Dylan realised they were shorts.

'We have to leave NOW!' Dylan shouted to his scaly friends.

The iguanas sprang into action. Well, Paul, Pauline and Smelly Paul sprang into action. Red-Eye was still very much asleep. He was dreaming of that time he defeated the Platypus Kid and had just got to the awesome part where he totally KADUNKA-CHUNKED a 10-foot platypus ...

Smelly Paul launched himself out of the cage and grabbed Dylan's rucksack from the wardrobe.

'DIVE! DIVE! DIVE!' Smelly Paul screamed.

Pauline jumped from the alarm clock into the bag. Smelly Paul crawled in, slow and stinky. Paul picked up Red-Eye and threw him in the air, before quickly climbing in himself. Red-Eye raised a foot as if he was performing a drop kick and landed in the bag, somehow remaining fast asleep.

Dylan had no time to change. He looked down to see that his shorts were stained with pizza grease and he was wearing odd socks – one green with stripes, the other red with Father Christmas on.

Dylan grabbed his rucksack and launched himself over the bannister, landing with his arm outstretched in true superhero fashion. He just managed to grab his sister's cape as she went to close the front door behind her.

'Errrrgh, he's holding onto my beautiful cape,' said Millie, her hands trying to prise off Dylan's fingers.

'We made it, Dylan, man,' Paul said, peeking his head out of the rucksack.

'I know we did, Paul.'

'It's so weird hearing you talk to your iguana friends, Dylan,' Sam said. 'It's a real shame you can't find any *real* ones.'

'Don't worry, Sam, when I become the world's most famous superhero, I will have too many to choose from. Besides, Paul, Pauline, Smelly Paul and Red-Eye Paul are all the friends I need,' he said, turning around to face his brother.

'HA! HA! HA!' Sam and Millie laughed uncontrollably. 'Oh, you look gorgeous, little bro. This is better, MUCH better than leaving him behind!' said Sam to Millie. He turned to his little brother and the iguanas, who were now on Dylan's shoulders in an act of solidarity, apart from Smelly Paul who was still asleep in the bottom of Dylan's rucksack. 'Onwards to Superhero HQ!'

8:03AM

High above the London skyline, right in between Big Ben and the London Eye is Superhero HQ. Now, those who have visited London (or have seen it in photographs or on a map) will probably be thinking, *No,*

it isn't. But whatever you might think, you are wrong. Superhero HQ *is* there, you just can't see it. The reason Ron Strongman had it designed with invisible glass was to keep all the evil supervillains away. Also, it's really cool to own a super-secret superhero hideout.

Millie, aka Millie Monday, and Sam, aka Arctic Thunder, landed next to Dylan on a flimsy cloud. The grand entrance to Superhero HQ was slowly beginning to materialise. It was truly spectacular, everything Dylan had ever imagined it would be and more.

'This is a one-time thing, kiddo,' said Arctic Thunder, who would only be referred

to as Sam at home.

'Yeah, don't get any ideas about travelling to work with us every day,' added Millie Monday.

'Or talking to us at work.'

'Or at home.'

'Just keep a low profile and don't get us into any trouble, OK? And find yourself a pair of shoes!'

'Lean over so I can bite his stupid nose again,' said Paul who was gritting his teeth and staring at Arctic Thunder.

'And keep that *thing* away from me,' said Arctic Thunder.

And, with that, Dylan's brother and sister flew on ahead through the large glass doors.

Inside the reception, everything was extraordinarily, dazzlingly white. The receptionist gave Dylan a confused look as he approached.

'Can I help you, Mr, Mr ...'

'Iguana Boy,' said Dylan, puffing out his chest

proudly. 'Ron Strongman's expecting me.'

'Oh, yes, Iguana Boy,' she said, clearly trying to hold in an epic laugh.

Paul was obviously excited to be there, he performed a series of backflips on the receptionist's desk.

'Wow, thanks for that,' she said, looking at Paul while thrusting a map of the building at Dylan. 'Iguana Boy, please, PLEASE do go up to the fifth floor immediately to find your office.'

On the fifth floor, Dylan passed his brother's office. He couldn't resist blowing a raspberry. Next up was Atomic Adam's, followed by his sister's. The door had a sign which said:

Turning a corner, he came across Terrifying Suzanne's office. The door was open so he tip-toed past.

'I SAID I WANTED RAISINS, THESE ARE SULTANAS, YOU FOOL!' she was screaming at a young boy.

'Here we are,' said Dylan, approaching another office door.

'Really?' asked Paul. 'Are you sure this is our office?'

Paul was so intrigued that he was standing on Dylan's head, obstructing the view with his tail. If Dylan could have seen through Paul (which would be a much COOLER

superpower than talking to him), he would have seen what looked like a long-forgotten coat cupboard. It was small. Really small. There were coat hooks lining the back wall, one tiny desk and one solitary chair.

But Dylan wouldn't let anything ruin his day. Who cared if he hadn't had time for a shower, was wearing cheese-stained shorts, odd socks, no shoes and a wet T-shirt, and had the world's smallest office?

'Well, it's not the biggest office, but nothing is going to spoil my first day as a superhero!' said Dylan unconvincingly, putting the rucksack down on the desk.

'Not the biggest, you say? That's the understatement of the century,' said Paul.

'This wouldn't be big enough for a five-year-old iguana's birthday party, let alone a ... wait, what are you again?' said Red-Eye. He had trouble remembering the different species of non-lizards.

'He's a human, you fool,' said Pauline.

'That's it, human. I always get you mixed up with those other things ... what are they called again?'

'Monkeys?' said Dylan.

'No, horses, silly.'

'It's an easy mistake to make,' added Smelly Paul in agreement.

Just as Dylan was beginning to relax, he heard a voice. 'Hey, who are you and who are you talking to?'

Dylan almost fell off the chair. 'Who is *that*? Where *are* you?' said Dylan. He and the iguanas looked around but they couldn't see anyone.

'I'm over here.'

'Or here.'

'Or maybe I'm here …'

The voice jumped around the room, never coming from the same place twice. It was very disorientating.

'Who are you talking to?' the voice asked again.

'My iguanas,' Dylan replied, still looking around the office.

'Easy, pal, we ain't *your* iguanas,' said Paul.

'Sorry, I mean *these* iguanas, who I do not own because they are their own beings,' Dylan corrected himself. Iguanas were very touchy about ownership.

'You can talk to iguanas?'

'Unfortunately ...'

Pauline bit Dylan's finger. 'Ouch!'

'That's pretty cool. Oh, I'm down here by the way.'

Dylan looked under the desk to see a boy smiling up at him. He had brown hair, which was neatly parted down the middle in the shape of curtains.

'I wanted to surprise you, we're desk buddies!' the boy said. 'Oh, and I suppose we're chair buddies too, there is only one of them, after all. Don't worry, I'll draw up a rota and we can share it! What's your name, stranger?'

'My name is Dylan Sp—' But before Dylan could finish, the boy had jumped up from under the desk and covered Dylan's mouth with the palm of his hand.

'Not your *real* name! No one is supposed to know your secret identity. Don't you know *anything* about being a superhero?'

'Yes, sorry. I'm Iguana Boy.'

'That's a cool name. Good to meet you. My name is VentriloChris. I can throw my voice like this.'

'Or this.'

'Or this'

'I'm sure you get the ...'

'Giiiiist.'

'Aren't you going to introduce me to your friends?'

'Sure,' said Dylan cautiously. He had been watching the Pauls' and Pauline's reactions to their new desk buddy and they didn't look best pleased.

'On my right shoulder is Paul.'

'I don't like this kid,' said Paul.

'Pleasure to meet you Paul,' said VentriloChris, extending a single finger to shake his claw. Paul declined.

'This one's friendly!' VentriloChris said. 'Paul, though ... what a strange name for an iguana ...'

'This here is Red-Eye Paul.'

'Another Paul? Crazy. Why do they call him, Red-Eye?' Dylan couldn't tell if he was joking. Red-Eye Paul's eye couldn't have been any redder ...

'Because he has a red eye ...'

'Ah yes, that would do it!' said VentriloChris, chuckling hysterically.

'Yep, I don't like him either' said Red-Eye.

'Next to him is Smelly Paul,' said Dylan.

'Well, colour me blue and call me a flamingo, another ruddy Paul! This is HILARIOUS!'

'It's a very popular name for an iguana,' said Dylan. 'And finally—'

'Let me guess,' said VentriloChris,

practically drooling at the prospect.

'I really wouldn't—' warned Dylan half-heartedly.

'You must be Paul!'

Pauline's face had turned a brighter red than Red-Eye Paul's eye. Without a moment's hesitation, she leapt across the table and slapped VentriloChris hard across the face with her tail.

'This is Pauline. She really doesn't like being called Paul.'

Just then, the door to the office opened, revealing a tall superhero dressed head to toe in black and holding a black leather coat.

'Be careful with this jacket, it's my favourite and the leather is particularly vulnerable to grease ...' he said, before casually placing the coat over Pauline and leaving.

'Oh yeah, that happens a lot. Some of the other superheroes seem to think this is the cloakroom,' VentriloChris explained.

Pauline managed to flick the coat off her back with an almighty swoop of her tail. The coat flew through the air and landed perfectly on one of the hooks.

Flick!!

'That. Was. INCREDIBLE!' shouted Red-Eye Paul who climbed up on to the table and gave her a high five.

'Nice flick' said Paul. 'Of course it was pure luck it landed on the hook, no way you meant that ...'

'Did too,' said Pauline, who appeared quite offended.

'Did not,' argued Smelly Paul.

'She did too,' said Red-eye Paul taking her side.

'Guys, it doesn't matter,' said Dylan

But it did matter to them. And sides had been taken, the line in the sand had been drawn ...

This was not how Dylan had expected his first day as a superhero to go.

REPEAT OFFENDER STRIKES AGAIN

10:59AM

The morning lingered like a bad smell. For once, it wasn't just down to Smelly Paul. Although it didn't help being trapped in a very small room with him.

Dylan had begun to welcome the

distraction of rude superheroes dropping off their coats. It gave him a brief interlude from VentriloChris' incessant talking.

'Hey, Iggy,' said VentriloChris. Dylan was in the office, and VentriloChris was at least fifty feet away down the corridor. Unfortunately, his voice hadn't stayed with him.

'I don't know what you're doing in there. Ron Strongman is giving a briefing right now and you're going to be late!' said VentriloChris in his highest voice.

Dylan gestured for the iguanas to get inside the rucksack quickly, before breaking into a run. He did not want to be late for his first-ever briefing with Ron Strongman. It was at times like this that he wished he had a more convenient superpower, such as super-speed.

By the time he reached the room, the door was closed. That was a bad sign. It meant the meeting must have already begun. VentriloChris was nowhere to be seen. *He must have made it in the nick of time*, Dylan thought.

'I made it just in the nick of time,' said VentriloChris, taunting him from the other side of the door.

Now, we have all at one time or another come across a creaky door. However, there isn't a door in existence creakier than the entrance to the briefing room at Superhero HQ. Some people suggested it had been designed that way to make latecomers feel incredibly awkward.

Before Dylan even turned the handle, the door creaked. Then the creak got louder and LOUDER until every eye in the room was on him.

Dylan slid through a narrow gap and closed the door behind him as quickly as possible.

'Sorry ...' he said to no one in particular. Millie Monday and Arctic Thunder were beaming. They loved nothing more than to see their little brother embarrassed.

'I'll continue, shall I?' said Ron, his eyes locked on Dylan. This was not how Dylan had wanted their first real meeting to go. In fact, he had been hoping to avoid Ron all day, given his attire, and to introduce himself the next day.

The floor was rammed full of superheroes, in every seat, in every row. There were even some heroes with flying powers hovering

above Dylan's head. Large screens hung from the ceiling and there, on a stage encrusted with disco lights, was Ron Strongman.

Ron Strongman. A man Dylan had idolised for years. The one who had noticed Iguana Boy for the hero he was and had invited him to join the Superhero Collective.

A man who ... was much, much smaller

than Dylan had expected. With a name like Strongman, a living legend with slicked-back hair and a silver goatee who had founded the Superhero Collective, Dylan had been expecting him to be tall. He had only ever seen him on screen before. He looked as if a stiff breeze (or a hearty sneeze) would blow him right over. But, what he lacked in physical strength, he clearly made up for with his BOOMING voice.

'As I was saying, before I was rudely interrupted,' Ron boomed, 'there is a supervillain causing havoc across London. A villain who goes by the name REPEAT OFFENDER.'

A collective gasp whooshed across the

room like an untied balloon. Dylan chuckled to himself, thinking that the gasp could probably blow Ron Strongman over.

'Repeat Offender has completely fooled the police, robbing bank after bank with no policeman able to stop his trickery. But more worryingly, he has got the better of us, and the awesome superheroes we have under our roof – the superheroes of Superhero HQ.'

Again, a collective gasp sounded in the auditorium.

'Now, I don't like to admit to this, but honestly, I'm impressed.'

There are certain things you should never say as a superhero:

1.

'HEY, I'M SAHARA SANDSTORM BUT MY REAL NAME IS GRACE PARK AND I LIVE AT 123 ST VINCENT STREET IN GLORIOUS FARNHAM.'

A superhero's secret identity is exactly that. A secret (otherwise it would be simply called an identity). It must be protected at all costs.

2.

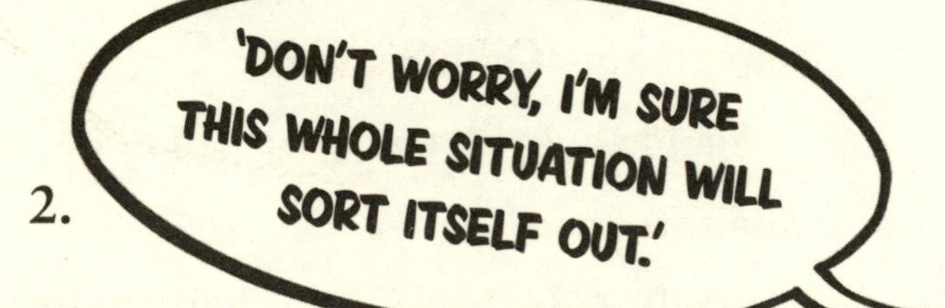

No it won't. That's why we have superheroes to sort things out. It doesn't matter what the situation is, if a superhero can get involved and make things better, they will. No crime is too small.

3.

A supervillain should never impress you, and even if they do, you should NEVER give them the satisfaction of knowing it.

4.

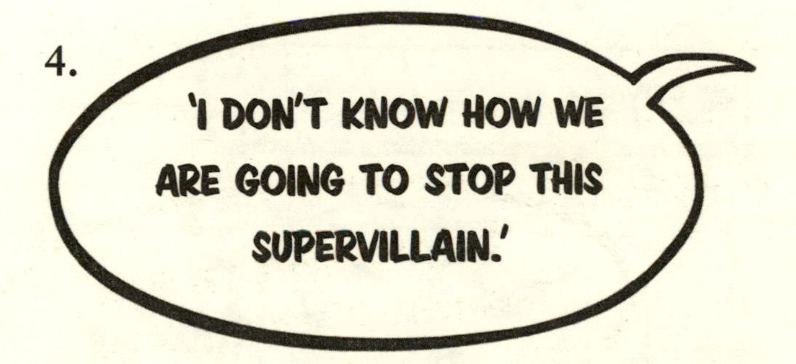

Well, now this is simply the worst thing you can say. A superhero must always have a plan. No villain, no matter how powerful is unstoppable.

'I don't know how we are going to stop this supervillain,' Ron Strongman continued. 'Just take a look at this footage of a robbery at the Royal Bank of London this morning ...' He signalled to his assistant to roll down the video screen.

ALARM
OW!
OOF!
OUCH!
RO
STOP RIGHT THERE SO I CAN CATCH YOU!
YOU AREN'T GOING TO CATCH ME. THIS ISN'T MY FIRST TIME DOING THIS.
WE KNOW ALL ABOUT YOUR LITTLE CRIME SPREE, REPEAT OFFENDER. LET'S JUST SAY ...
I WON'T BE REPEATING ANY MORE CRIMES WHERE I'M GOING ... YES, YES, YES I'VE HEARD IT ALL BEFORE.

YOUR TIME IS UP REPEAT OFFENDER.
WAIT ... WHERE IS HE?
I'M RIGHT ABOVE YOU. HAVE A NICE TRIP.
OOF!
WAIT, WHAT DO YOU ..?
THANK YOU FOR THE EXPLOSIVE EXIT, ATOMIC ADAM. I'VE ALWAYS WANTED TO BE A HIGH-FLYING CRIMINAL. CATCH YOU LATER ...

'As you can see, this morning, Repeat Offender defied not only the police, but our very own Atomic Adam,' said Ron Strongman.

'I've never been so humiliated,' said Atomic Adam, from the front row, his fists tightening.

'How much did he steal?' asked a superhero with a bright-pink cape.

'Yes, well, I don't think the amount is the issue here,' said Atomic Adam, whose face was growing redder by the second.

'Five pounds,' said Ron Strongman to stunned silence.

'Five pounds? Just five quid? Did he get disturbed whilst he was in the vault?' piped up Lacey Shoestring, Dylan's brother's favourite superhero.

'Actually, no,' said Arctic Thunder as he flew up to the stage, taking the opportunity to answer her question himself. 'Repeat Offender entered the vault completely undetected. He then took a single five pound note and put it in his pocket, before activating the alarm.'

'He activated the alarm himself? To steal FIVE POUNDS?' shouted someone from the crowd, causing more people to voice their opinions.

'That much effort for so little dough?'

'Where's the wonga?'

'The dosh.'

'The notes.'

'The scratch.'

'The cheese.'

'Show. Me. The. Spondoolicks!'

Each of these voices was actually VentriloChris who enjoyed stirring a crowd into frenzy whenever he got the chance.

'Silence, all of you!' boomed Ron, receiving instant compliance. 'I have no idea what "spondoolicks" are, but I understand your frustrations. I don't like being made to look foolish any more than the rest of you, but this is no ordinary supervillain we are dealing with.'

'WHAT CAN THIS FOOL DO?' screamed Terrifying Suzanne.

'We don't know,' said Ron. 'Looking at the tapes of all of his robberies, there doesn't seem to be any particular superpower on show. He is a very smooth operator, always one step ahead of the police and now, unfortunately, us too.

'I want you ALL to push your superpowers to their limits. We need to find out what supervillain powers Repeat Offender has – then, we must put him behind bars.'

Dylan had been listening intently to what Ron Strongman had to say. He removed his backpack from his shoulder and whispered inside, 'This is our chance to show Ron Strongman EXACTLY what we can do.'

'And what EXACTLY is it that a new

superhero and four iguanas CAN do?' asked Paul.

'We are going to find this Repeat Offender and we are going to stop him!'

PARKPUMP FITNESS MEMBERSHIP CARD
NAME: ZACHARY WOODWARD-LAMBERT
AKA: REPEAT OFFENDER
SUPERPOWER: TURNING BACK TIME (BY 30 SECONDS)
AGE/HEIGHT: 9yrs/4ft
DISGUISE: YELLOW CAPE
WEAKNESS: BEING CLUMSY

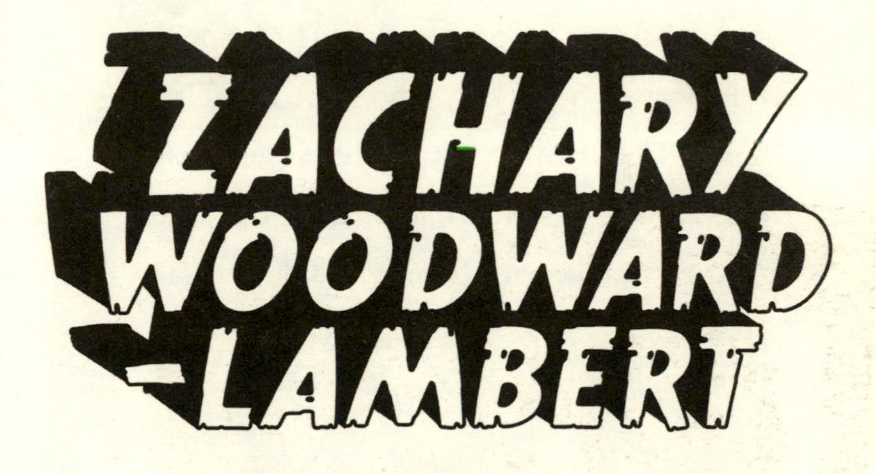

Long before there was Repeat Offender, there was a boy called Zachary Woodward-Lambert. Sole heir to the vast Woodward-Lambert empire, which was built upon a strange fitness regime his parents had started in a park many years ago. (Zac didn't understand people's obsession with getting

fit in increasingly bizarre fashion, but it certainly made his parents A LOT of money.)

He was a quiet kid, who kept himself to himself. He had to, really, because he was EXTRAORDINARILY clumsy, and when he tried to mix with others, it didn't usually go well ...

A FEW YEARS AGO ...
WELL DONE, HEIDI!
A,B,C
SORRY ...

LAST YEAR ...
MAY I HAVE A PIECE OF BREAD PLEASE?
SNAP!
SORRY...

LAST WEEK ...
'COULD YOU THROW US THE BALL PLEASE, ZAC?'
FISH 'n' CHIPS
BANG!
NO FISH 'n' CHIPS
SORRY ...

It was for all these reasons and more that Zac kept himself to himself at school. Ultimately, it was to protect everyone else's safety. But one day, all that changed, as he took the first step towards becoming Repeat Offender, the world's most loved supervillain.

It was like any other lunchtime at school; most of the boys were playing football on the field, destroying their smart black shoes and getting grass stains all over their uniforms.

Zac would often watch, wishing he could get involved. It wasn't like he hadn't tried. He had played football before, but he wasn't very good. He would invariably be put in goal and he had never saved a single shot (which made some kids VERY angry). Also, the ball seemed attracted to his face!

He always ended up making a fool of himself, so in the end he decided it was best not to try. Instead, he would spend his lunch breaks sitting all alone reading a book. Then one day, one of the girls from his class came and sat down next to him.

'What are you reading?' said the cool girl. She had long brown hair with a pair of bright-pink sunglasses balanced on top of her head.

'I'm ... uh ...'

'OK, I can see I've caught you off guard. Let's rewind. It's nice to meet you.'

'I'm ... uh ... Za ... Za ...'

‘Zaza? I do know your name, Zachary, or do you prefer to be called Zac?’

‘Yes …’

‘Yes, you prefer Zac?’

‘I’m Zac.’

‘OK, good, we’re getting somewhere.

Feeling up to telling me what you're reading?'

'A book,' said Zac, who was now sweating so much he was having to frantically blink water out of his eyes.

'Yes, what book? I like to read too. My favourite book is *The Pumpkin Project*. Have you read that?'

'I ... uh ... I'm reading a book on time-travelling aliens,' said Zac in what is to this day the longest sentence he has ever said to a girl.

'Oh ... that's kinda cute, I guess.'

At this point, other kids across the playground began to notice the exchange.

Soon a group of kids had surrounded them on the bench.

'Zac has a girlfriend!' shouted one of the boys.

'Urgh, why are you talking to *him*? He's such a weirdo,' added one of the girls. Before long, everyone was pointing at them and laughing.

Finally, just as Zac got up, two boys ran over with a large bucket of water and threw it over both of them. The cool girl ran off in tears, leaving Zac wishing that the ground would open up and swallow him.

Everyone has wished they could turn back time at one point in their lives – if only by thirty seconds to stop something embarrassing happening, like having a huge bucket of water thrown over you and someone you like.

Only on this occasion,

when nine-year-old Zac looked down at his watch and made the wish, that's exactly what happened.

'OK, good, we're getting somewhere. Feeling up to telling me what you're reading?' said the cool girl, for what Zac was fairly sure was the second time. He froze, only this time it wasn't because he was nervous. He was confused.

'What's wrong? Are you OK?' she asked.

'Sorry, déjà vu,' said Zac, not entirely convinced.

'Zac has a girlfriend!' shouted one of the boys.

'Urgh, why are you talking to *him*? He's such a weirdo,' added one of the girls.

'No, please don't,' said Zac, moving swiftly out of the way without thinking. Water came crashing down all over the cool girl, missing him by a matter of millimetres.

'What is going on?' he said, looking down at his watch.

'OK good, we're getting somewhere. Feeling up to telling me what you're reading?' said the girl once more. They were sitting on the same bench, but this was definitely not the first time Zac had been here. Yet for the cool girl, well, it seemed to be.

'I'm reading a book on time-travelling aliens,' replied Zac almost involuntarily. It was as if it was a script. He knew what was coming next.

'That's kinda—'

'Cute,' interrupted Zac. This was the first time he had ever finished someone else's train of thought (it was pretty easy to do when you had already heard it).

'Yes, that's exactly what I was going to say!'

'Zac has a girlfriend!' shouted one of the boys.

'Urgh, why are you talking to *him*? He's such a weirdo,' added one of the girls.

Zac jumped up and tried to get to the cool

girl before the water hit them, but he didn't move fast enough and they both ended up in a wet heap on the floor. He spent the next three hours going back to try to protect them both but no matter what he did, the cool girl always ended up getting soaked. In the end, he had an idea.

'OK good, we're getting somewhere. Feeling up to telling me what you're reading?' said the cool girl.

'LEAVE ME ALONE!' Zac erupted, jumping up onto the seat and pointing at her.

The cool girl burst into tears and ran over to her friends who consoled her at the same time as shooting Zac disapproving glances.

He still looked like a drowned rat and got soaked with a bucket of water, but at least she didn't.

The girl had spent no more than a minute or two with Zac, but he had spent hours with her, with someone who was just trying to be his friend. And now his public image at school was the worst it had ever been. But not for long.

Zac suddenly saw the beauty of being able to rewind time by thirty seconds. No one ever saw anything other than what he wanted them to see. All the right moves, at exactly the right time. It looked effortless. All he had to do was rewind time.

11:15AM

After the briefing, Dylan found VentriloChris outside the office door with a box of stuff in his hands.

'Looks like you finally caught a break, kid,' said Paul, clapping his claws together

approvingly on Dylan's shoulder. 'It looks like Chris is leaving,' he whispered.

'What's going on?' Dylan asked.

VentriloChris didn't say A SINGLE WORD as Dylan approached. Behind him, Dylan could see a very angry looking Terrifying Suzanne standing in their office.

VentriloChris shot his hand back, holding out his phone to Dylan, who looked down to see an email:

TO: VentriloChris

FROM: R.STRONGMAN

Dear VentriloChris,

Some offices here at Superhero HQ have become a little cramped. I know, I was deeply upset on hearing this too.

BUT have no fear! A solution has been found. All we have had to do is move around a few superheroes to make life easier for EVERYONE.

You see, Arctic Thunder's office simply isn't big enough for a superhero of his stature. After all, he has won the Superstar award every month this year. It has come to my attention that he has only ONE water cooler and NO private bathroom. I know, I too was mortified to learn of this.

To rectify this issue, we have knocked a wall down into another room and relocated the previous occupant to your office.

I'm sure you understand,

Ron Strongman
C.E.O

PS It's Terrifying Suzanne.

Dylan looked at VentriloChris in amazement as he handed his phone back. The iguanas were clinging to his back, trying to avoid eye contact with Terrifying Suzanne.

'What did it say?' asked Smelly Paul.

'It said that Terrifying Suzanne is moving into our office because my brother needed more space in his office!' said Dylan.

'WHAT?!' Pauline gasped.

'Apparently he needed space for a SECOND water cooler.'

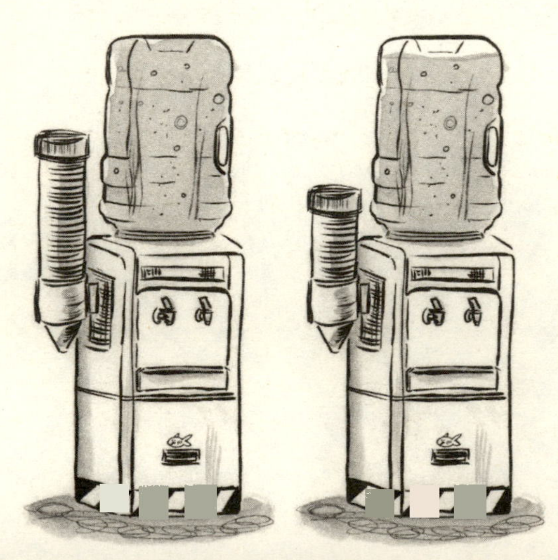

'But he is Arctic Thunder. The only superhero who can create water from his fingertips,' said Paul.

'Man, it's going to smell *really* bad in there with all the extra people ...' said Smelly Paul, holding his nose. The other iguanas were in too much shock to point out the irony of this statement. A few minutes went by where neither VentriloChris nor Dylan had the nerve to enter the room.

'Look who it is, if it isn't my favourite superhero, Iguana Kid!' said Arctic Thunder, flying down the corridor, wearing the smuggest smile that Dylan had ever seen. 'Ah, I see you have met your new roomie. Don't worry she doesn't bite.'

'This was your doing, wasn't it Sam?' asked Dylan.

'Me?' asked Arctic Thunder, pointing to himself and acting shocked. 'All I said to our wonderful leader Mr Strongman was that being a superhero is thirsty work. I'm often parched after a hard day saving the world.' He put his hand to his throat and started to cough slowly. 'See, my throat is as dry as the Sahara Desert right now. That's why I needed a water cooler.'

'A *second* water cooler,' Dylan corrected him.

Arctic Thunder took out a plastic cup from his bag and filled it with water from his hand as if by magic. He took a large gulp and sighed with satisfaction.

'Ice cold, every single time. Anyway I can't hang about with my baby brother all day, people to save, supervillains to catch, awards to win ... You know how it is. Well, you don't and never will but ... Enjoy your day. Well, I mean have an awful day ...' He popped his head around the door and looked inside the 'office'. 'Ooh, spacious!'

Terrifying Suzanne flicked him right on the nose, causing him to fly up and hit his head on the ceiling. Despite the obvious pain he was in, Sam simply flew back down the corridor laughing.

'Right, I'm going in,' said VentriloChris, although his legs didn't actually move.

'WHAT DO YOU MEAN I HAVE TO SHARE AN OFFICE? WHO ARE THESE FOOLS?' shouted Terrifying Suzanne, so loudly, in fact, that VentriloChris wondered if she, too, could throw her voice.

Dylan couldn't take the tension anymore and decided to enter the office. 'Hi, Terrifying Suzanne,' he said. 'Not sure if you remember me, but we were once locked together in a prison cell by an evil supervillain called the Platypus Kid, before we broke out and I saved the world with my iguanas?'

Terrifying Suzanne stared at Dylan without saying a word.

'Ooh, oh, tell her about the bit where I was all like, K'POW!' said Red-Eye, completely failing to read the situation.

'I don't think that would help,' whispered Dylan. 'OK, not ringing any bells? That's cool, let's start over. My name is Iguana Boy, but my friends call me Dylan.'

'How many times do I have to tell you, your secret identity—'

Dylan ignored VentriloChris and aimed his best smile at Terrifying Suzanne, hoping to receive a smile back. Or a nod. Or even a grunt.

A couple of superheroes approached the office (cupboard. It was really just a cupboard). Dylan had never seen superhero twins before. They both wore tight white leather trousers and black tank tops and carried black and white leather jackets. Dylan could just make out some kind of emblem emblazoned on the backs. The only discernible difference was their hair. One had long, dark-purple braids and the other

TELEPATHY
TWINS

had red ones.

They held out their jackets to Dylan. He flipped them over and saw that on the back of one jacket was the word TELEPATHY and on the other TWINS. He was about to return their garments and kindly inform them that this was not a cloakroom when the jackets disappeared from his hands. He looked down to see Pauline and Paul with the jackets draped over their tails.

'OK, on the count of three, launch those coats!' said Crazy Red-Eye Paul, rubbing his claws together excitedly.

'One ...'

'Uh ... guys ...' said Dylan.

'Two ...'

'What are you doing?' added Dylan before suddenly realising. 'Wait … no …'

'THREE!'

Pauline flicked her tail and the jacket with the word TWINS emblazoned on its back flew through the air, over the table, past a lamp which didn't look like it was plugged in, and landed perfectly on the hook at the back of the room.

Paul had also flicked his tail. The jacket with the word TELEPATHY on it hadn't gone quite as far. Or as high. BUT it had landed … over Terrifying Suzanne's head.

Paul froze in fear as Pauline and Red-Eye Paul celebrated. Terrifying Suzanne sat motionless, the word TELEPATHY perfectly displayed on the jacket that hung from her head.

With Terrifying Suzanne now physically unable to stare at him, Dylan used the opportunity to introduce himself to his utterly bewildered visitors.

'Hi there, my name is Dy ... Iguana Boy, it's a pleasure to meet you,' said Dylan.

'I'm Iffi and this is Fifi.'

'I can speak for myself.'

'It's just quicker if I introduce both of us.'

'But then no one remembers me, they only remember your name. Why can't it be Fifi and Iffi anyway?'

'Because it sounds stupid that way round.'

'Hello?' said Dylan.

'IT DOES NOT! Fifi and Iffi is much nicer. Besides, it's alphabetically correct. It goes f, g, h, i ...'

'Well maybe it's about time I was a little bit higher.'

'I SAID HELLO!' Dylan lost his cool and raised his voice. This was very rare.

'What?' said Iffi and Fifi at the same time, turning to face Dylan.

'I introduced myself, then I asked your names and you have just been staring at each other for the last two minutes.'

'Oh really?'

'Ah, we sometimes do that don't we, Iffi ...? Think we are talking out loud but actually we're just reading each other's minds ...'

'Oh yeah, good point Fifi.'

'You're doing it again now!'

'Oh sorry,' said Iffi, this time out loud so everyone else could hear. 'We really have to concentrate to make sure we are actually speaking rather than reading each other's minds.'

'YES. WE. DO,' said Fifi, very slowly and deliberately. 'That *was* out loud, right?' she added.

'Yes. It. Was. My name is VentriloChris by the way,' said VentriloChris, sending his voice all over the corridor. They were clearly impressed.

'Hey, that's pretty cool,' said Iffi.

'Thank you,' said VentriloChris.

Just what Dylan needed – more strange superheroes to join the party, AND they were all getting on with each other. Though, Terrifying Suzanne still hadn't moved, and Dylan was beginning to worry that she had been rendered motionless with rage. A rage that would eventually erupt …

'Say, Telepathy Twins, any chance you could read her mind right now, let us all know what she's thinking?' asked VentriloChris, gesturing at Terrifying Suzanne.

'Yeah, about that, we can't read other people's minds, just each other's,' said Fifi.

Dylan wondered how on earth the Telepathy Twins had made it into the Superhero Collective. They must have saved the world at some point, it was the only way to be inducted, but if they found it this difficult to have a fairly simple conversation, how on earth did they manage to SAVE THE WORLD?

'HOW DARE YOU THROW A COAT ON ME? GO AWAY, YOU FOOLS!' bellowed Terrifying Suzanne suddenly. She yelled with such force, the coat flew off her head and landed neatly on the hook next to the TWINS jacket. Pauline gave her an approving nod.

Dylan was pretty sure that Terrifying Suzanne didn't have the power to control people's minds, yet almost as soon as the words had escaped her mouth, she got her wish – the new office residents dispersed.

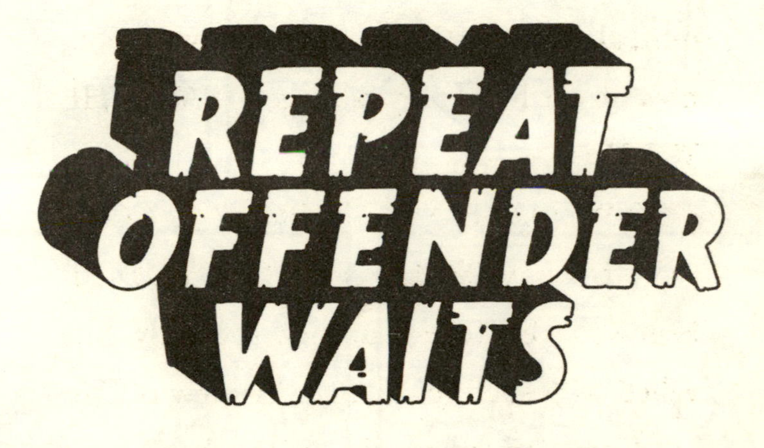

Everything had gone EXACTLY how Repeat Offender had planned. He had entered the bank, made his way to the vault, set off the alarm, grabbed a five-pound note and made his way back to the entrance.

BANK
OOH, LOOK AT THE BIG PLANE!

ARE YOU OK, SIR?
BANG!

QUITE ALL RIGHT THANK YOU.
I JUST NEED TO ... USE THE BATHROOM.

VAULT
IS HE OK?
I'M NOT SURE, HE WON'T STOP CRYING!
RO

MONEY
£5
RO
ALARM LEVER
MONEY

ALARM
£5
RO
ALARM
£5
RO
ALARM
£5
ALARM
£5

11:30am

'ALERT. ALERT. A SUPERVILLAIN IS CAUSING CHAOS SOMEWHERE. REPORT TO THE BRIEFING ROOM. ALERT. ALERT.'

‘Oh my days, this is our big chance,’ said Iffi who had just joined Dylan’s table at the canteen with her sister to get away from Terrifying Suzanne.

‘Looks like you aren’t the only one desperate to prove yourself, dude,’ said Paul.

Dylan and the rest of his gang ran towards the briefing room as fast as they could. He opened the door once more to an almighty creak and slipped inside. Everyone turned and looked at the group disapprovingly, including Ron Strongman, who Dylan had clearly interrupted once again.

‘Sorry,’ said Dylan to no one in particular.

‘Shall I continue?’ said Ron Strongman, this time very clearly to Dylan. Dylan nodded meekly.

'Right, time is of the essence, we have a Code 87 Magenta underway at the Greater London Bank.'

'Are you sure, sir?' said Arctic Thunder.

'Of course I'm sure! We need to send our top heroes there immediately.'

'In that case, I suggest we send Iguana Boy,' Arctic said.

A gasp rippled across the crowd, steadily turning into a mixture of laughter and people mumbling, 'Who's that?'

Dylan could just make out Millie smiling encouragingly.

What was going on?

His brother had actually put him forwards

for a mission and his sister was happy about it. He couldn't believe it.

'Yes, well ...' said Ron Strongman clearing his throat. 'Of course, I trust your impeccable intuition, Arctic Thunder, however Repeat Offender has already seen off far more experienced superheroes, such as Atomic Adam, and I fear—'

'Oh!' said Arctic Thunder, clapping his hands together dramatically, 'You mean a Code 88 Maroon: an evil supervillain is attempting a bank robbery.'

'Yes, of course, what did I say?'

'A Code 87 Magenta: a cat stuck in a very low tree ...'

The laughter was the loudest Dylan had

heard all day. Despite the seriousness of the crime currently taking place, even Ron Strongman allowed himself a chuckle.

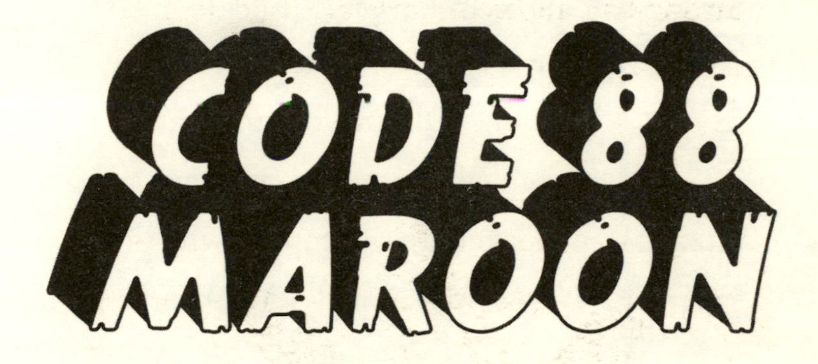

12:15am

Arctic Thunder and the rest of the superheroes Ron Strongman had sent out on Code 88 Maroon arrived at the bank too late. Repeat Offender was nowhere to be seen.

On a roof opposite the building,

Repeat Offender was watching, casually folding the five-pound note he had stolen into a paper aeroplane. He threw it off the roof without looking, and it landed perfectly in the top pocket of the father who was now desperately walking up and down outside the bank with the buggy, trying to calm his little boy down.

He took it out of his pocket and opened it up. Scribbled on one side was a note saying,

'BUY THE KID AN ICE CREAM ALREADY!'

The father looked around aimlessly, before walking away from the bank.

Repeat Offender could see that the superheroes had eventually arrived, long after he had made it out of the bank and to the top of the building opposite. They were only there for a short time, and looked far from happy when they left. It was enough to convince him that they hadn't been planning a clever trap. They were just really, really late ...

Each time he robbed a bank, the result was the same. They looked stupid, and he looked cool. Once again, he had committed a crime and no one had been able to stop him.

By the time he had returned home it was all over the news.

'BREAKING NEWS, EVERYONE'S FAVOURITE SUPERVILLAIN HAS STRUCK AGAIN, THIS TIME AT THE GREATER LONDON BANK. THE SUPERHERO COLLECTIVE WERE SLOW TO REACT, AND THE SUPERCOOL SUPERVILLAIN ONCE MORE MANAGED TO AVOID DETECTION, MAKING OFF WITH A SINGLE FIVE-POUND NOTE. MAN, THAT MUST REALLY IRRITATE THOSE GUYS AND GALS OVER AT SUPERHERO HQ!'

said the newsreader, chuckling to himself.

Repeat Offender turned off the TV.

'Everyone's favourite supervillain,' he said to himself thoughtfully. 'I like that.'

You're probably thinking, *Why would a supervillain care about his popularity? Surely he should be concentrating on taking over the world? And why does he only take five pounds, that's not going to buy him a super-duper, laser shooter, deathray, X-Ray, doomsday device* ... And you would be right, most supervillains are obsessed with world domination and material possessions, but Repeat Offender was no ordinary supervillain. He sighed as he thought about how exhausting it was keeping up with the demands of being a super-cool supervillain. Repeat Offender. He closed his eyes and thought back to his very first bank heist of the day ...

HEY! YOU'RE THAT SUPERVILLAIN, REPEAT OFFENDER. YOU'RE NOT STEALING ANYTHING FROM THIS BANK LAD.
VAULT
30 SECOND REWIND
OW, OW, OW! SECURITY GUARD TO THE LEFT, 5 PACES.
GOOD MORNING DOLORES, YOU ARE LOOKING BEAUTIFUL THIS MORNING, AS ALWAYS.
WHY THANK YOU VERY MUCH, DON.
VAULT
HEY! YOU'RE THAT SUPERVILLAIN, REPEAT OFFENDER. YOU'RE NOT STEALING ANYTHING FROM THIS BANK LAD.
VAULT
2000
LOCKED
OK, OK, YOU GOT ME, BUT NOT THE EAR PLEASE!
WAIT HOW DID YOU ...
30 SECOND REWIND
LOVELY TALKING TO YOU DOLORES, BUT I MUST DO MY ROUNDS AND CHECK ON THE VAULT.
UNLOCKED

A LITTLE WHILE LATER ...
LOCKED
VAULT
ALARM
OH, WOW! THAT IS A LOT OF POLICE OFFICERS ...
HANDS IN THE AIR KID.
THIS IS GOING TO BE DIFFICULT ...
THREE HUNDRED ATTEMPTS LATER ...
30
STOP RIGHT THERE SO I CAN CATCH YOU!

BUMP!!
OW!! THAT REALLY HURT YOU KNOW ...
30 SECOND REWIND
STOP RIGHT THERE SO I CAN CATCH YOU.
YOU AREN'T GOING TO CATCH ME. THIS ISN'T MY FIRST TIME DOING THIS.
WE KNOW ALL ABOUT YOUR LITTLE CRIME SPREE REPEAT OFFENDER. LET'S JUST SAY YOU WON'T BE REPEATING ANY MORE CRIMES WHERE YOU'RE GOING ...

ATOMIC ADAM WALKS IN.
YOUR TIME IS UP REPEAT OFFENDER.
(ATOMIC'S BELLYBUTTON FLUFF)
BANG!
OUCH!
30 SECOND REWIND
YEP, THAT ONE HURT THE MOST.
WE KNOW ALL ABOUT YOUR LITTLE CRIME SPREE REPEAT OFFENDER. LET'S JUST SAY ...
I WON'T BE REPEATING ANY MORE CRIMES WHERE I'M GOING ... YES, YES, YES, I'VE HEARD IT ALL BEFORE.
I'M RIGHT ABOVE YOU.
YOUR TIME IS UP REPEAT OFFENDER. WAIT ... WHERE IS HE?
OH, GREAT. LET'S GET YOU DOWN SHALL WE?
(MORE BELLYBUTTON FLUFF)
BANG!
30 SECOND REWIND
DO YOU HAVE ANY IDEA HOW MUCH IT HURTS TO REPEATEDLY FALL FROM A GREAT HEIGHT?!

PHEWF! THAT'LL DO.

02:30pm

All the superheroes and the world press had gathered in the briefing room at Superhero HQ to hear Ron Strongman deliver a press conference – something he only did when things were really bad. Dylan had thankfully

made it on time and was sitting next to VentriloChris waiting to hear the latest news on Repeat Offender.

'Thank you for gathering here today. I would like to make a short statement and then I will take a few questions,' said Ron Strongman in a very serious tone. 'Today, the supervillain known as Repeat Offender struck another two banks, putting innocent members of the public in serious danger. Unfortunately, the Superhero Collective was unable to apprehend him, and he escaped once more. To the nation, I say this. Do not panic. We are here to protect you and keep you safe and that is what we will do.

'And to Repeat Offender,' he continued,

looking directly down the lenses of the cameras 'hear me when I say, we will find you. We will capture you. And we will bring you to justice.'

There was a mild round of applause – the superheroes knew not to get too excited in front of the press. Then the questions came thick and fast ...

'You've been saying you're going to capture him for three weeks now, when are you going to ACTUALLY do it?'

'As soon as we possibly can.'

'Your superheroes didn't even make it to the bank before he had left the last robbery, would you agree that Repeat Offender has taken a few steps even further ahead of you?'

'For every step forward, he will ultimately end up taking two steps back.'

'If you could turn back time and do things differently, what would you change? And a follow up question, if you went back in time and did something differently, and Repeat Offender STILL had the better of you, what ELSE would you change when you went back in time for a second time because you failed miserably the first time?'

'The second time I wouldn't have let you ask such a foolish question. Thank you for your time, that will be all,' said Ron Strongman, walking off stage.

It was everything Ron Strongman had come to expect from the press. When the

Superhero Collective were saving the world they were full of praise, when they weren't ... well, they could be pretty horrible, dragging their good name through the mud.

Dylan could wait in the wings no longer. During the press conference he had made a decision. He would go and speak directly to Ron Strongman, and ask for his permission to bring Repeat Offender to justice ... with the help of his trusty iguanas, of course.

TIME FOR POOP

02:45pm

It took Dylan much longer to find Ron Strongman's office than he had expected. It was buried away at the end of another impossibly long corridor, and there were no signs to point you in the right direction. It

was almost as if he didn't want to be found.

Dylan knocked on the door but there was no answer. He knocked again, this time opening the door ever so slightly. He wasn't in the least bit surprised to hear it creak.

'Excuse me, Mr Strongman ...'

'Yes, yes, come on in,' said Ron Strongman, not looking up from his tablet. He was staring intently at it, looking rather troubled.

The room was huge. It made Dylan's office look like a cupboard. Actually Dylan's office WAS a cupboard, so it made his office look like a small wardrobe. Dylan also wasn't the slightest bit surprised to see THREE water coolers.

'If this is a bad time ...'

'Nonsense, kid, come here. I'm just having a little trouble destroying a guerilla army that is threatening to take over a local government.'

'Oh wow, that definitely sounds more important, I'll go—'

'NO!' shouted Ron, smashing his fist down on to his desk. 'It would appear I am dead,' he said, turning the tablet around to show an image of a cartoon Ron Strongman lying on the floor with the words "You Died" written in goofy blood.

'Oh, it's a game. I see.'

'Not just a game, kid, helps develop my strategic mind.' Ron looked up for the first time and frowned. 'What on earth are you wearing?'

'I had a few wardrobe issues this morning, you see my brother was rushing me while I was getting dressed ...'

'Yes, yes I have a brother or two, or three ... Yes I think it's three, so I know exactly what you're talking about. Hijinks, I believe we called it in my day. Anyway, the name is Ron Strongman, pleasure to meet you.'

'We have met over video link before.'

'Yes, of course! Uh ...' said Ron, waving his hand and stretching out the "uh" as if Dylan's name was on the tip of his tongue and at any moment it would come back to him (they both knew it wasn't coming back to him).

'Iguana Boy,' said Dylan, giving up as per usual. 'It's my first day today.'

'Iguana Kid, of course! How have you been, having a great first day I expect?'

Dylan ignored the incorrect name, but Paul couldn't. He climbed out of Dylan's backpack and rested on his shoulders, despite Dylan having asked him to stay hidden. 'Firstly, sir,' Dylan began, 'I would like to apologise on behalf of myself and my iguana friends here for interrupting your briefing this morning.'

'Don't apologise!' said Paul 'He doesn't even remember your name. That's very rude, you know, think of how angry Pauline gets when people get HER name wrong ...'

Paul kept talking to Dylan, and was rustling around on his shoulder, scratching his chin with his foot and generally just being VERY distracting.

Dylan tried to ignore it and act professional.

'Interrupt my briefing, did you?' Continued Ron Strongman, looking completely unfazed by Paul's presence. 'Yes, well, of course I do remember that happening, and you, I remember you too, so … don't do it again, kid.'

'I won't, sir, I will never be late again, I promise.'

'Good to hear, Iguana Kid.'

'I'm a bit offended you don't remember me. I saved the world once!'

'HA! Once?! Really? Well, bravo Lizard boy. Once is a given, you wouldn't be allowed in the building if you hadn't saved the world at least once. You realise that most of the superheroes here save the world *once a day*?'

'Hey, this is only his first day!' said Paul, jumping to Dylan's defence. He directed his words at Ron Strongman. Not that he could hear them of course.

'And the day isn't over YET, Mr Don Wronghands. Yeah, that's right, I got your name wrong, pal, doesn't feel good, does it?'

'Look, all I have wanted to be ever since I could remember is a superhero. I finally developed my power, worked hard and was personally invited to the Superhero Collective by my hero. You!' Dylan sighed heavily.

'And now I'm having the worst day of my life. But you know what, I could take it all: the laughter at my terrible taste in clothes, the tiny office I'm sharing with two crazy superheroes –'

'Where people think you are a cloakroom attendant,' added Paul.

'All the other superheroes just think I am a cloakroom attendant,' said Dylan. 'I could take the humiliation if I was allowed to go out on just one simple mission. My iguanas and I might just have the power needed to stop Repeat Offender in his tracks.'

'It was pretty brave to stand up to me like that. Not many people do. I see real potential in you, Iguana Kid,' said Ron Strongman, looking at Dylan properly for the first time.

Dylan was so happy to hear words of encouragement that he didn't even mind that he had been called the wrong name.

'I haven't sent you on any missions,' said Ron, 'because a superhero with your kind of power ... wait, what is it you can do again?'

'I can talk to iguanas.'

'Exactly, talk to iguanas, with a power such as ...' He froze mid-sentence and stared at Dylan, releasing a small laugh. 'You talk to iguanas – the little lizard creatures like that one on your shoulder?'

Paul dug his claws into Dylan's shoulder to show his disapproval. 'Well, I don't think they would like being referred to as ...' Dylan paused. 'Yes the little lizard creatures.'

'Yes, yes, well, with a power like ... that ... well, I have created a very important department and I want YOU to head it up.'

'Wow! *Really?* An entire department to myself?' Dylan asked. 'I don't know if I'm quite ready for that.'

'You were born ready, Lizard Boy. You may not be aware, but right now POOP is causing me a lot of trouble.'

Dylan looked at Ron blankly, trying not to laugh. Surely he had misheard. 'I'm sorry, did you say POOP?'

'What's wrong with you, kid, never heard of POOP before? You're POOP, I'm POOP, this whole building is full of POOP.'

'I'm not following you.'

'Don't you read your emails? I sent one out after the press conference. We are no longer the Superhero Collective, we are now POOP,' said Ron Strongman, seeming oblivious as to why Dylan was having a hard time understanding this.

'Yes, yes,' Ron continued. 'It's a little trick I learnt, you see, whenever the organisation goes through a bit of a hard time, I hold a press conference and change the name of the company. Everyone will be so distracted about the company name change that they won't be so obsessed with our little problem, Repeat Offender, who is making us look like fools EVERY DAY. Yes, it really would be better if he at least stole more money than a fiver. It's embarrassing not to be able to catch a supervillain who steals such a small amount of wonga.'

'So, you're turning us into POOP?' asked Dylan sarcastically.

'Exactly! You got it. I knew I was making

the right decision here. Yes, as we speak we are covering our uniforms, walls, stationery, anything we can get hold of in POOP, but that will only go so far.'

'I really hope he means a logo,' said Paul, holding his nose.

'I understand,' Dylan said, still trying not to laugh. 'We need to tackle the problem head-on and you believe that I can lead the team to capture Repeat Offender. I won't let you down, sir.'

'Not exactly, Iguana Kid,' said Ron, bursting his bubble. He walked around the side of his desk and perched on the corner, arms folded. 'I'm sure your brother Arctic Thunder has that covered with his amazing superpowers to create thunderstorms from his fingertips. What I need from you is in some ways more important. I need a superhero willing to improve the image of POOP.'

'There is only so much you can do to make POOP look good ...'

'Yes, yes, and I think you're the boy to do it. Make us look nice and shiny once again. That's why I'm putting you in charge of the CITD.'

Dylan wasn't great with acronyms (in fact he didn't even know they were called acronyms), and he had no idea what Ron Strongman was talking about. However, he was suddenly in a better mood. He had just been put in charge of the CITD (whatever that meant) at POOP (whatever that meant) on his very first day as a superhero, and he wasn't going to let anything get in the way of his brand new promotion.

'Thank you, sir, I won't let you down,' said Dylan, shaking Ron Strongman's hand enthusiastically.

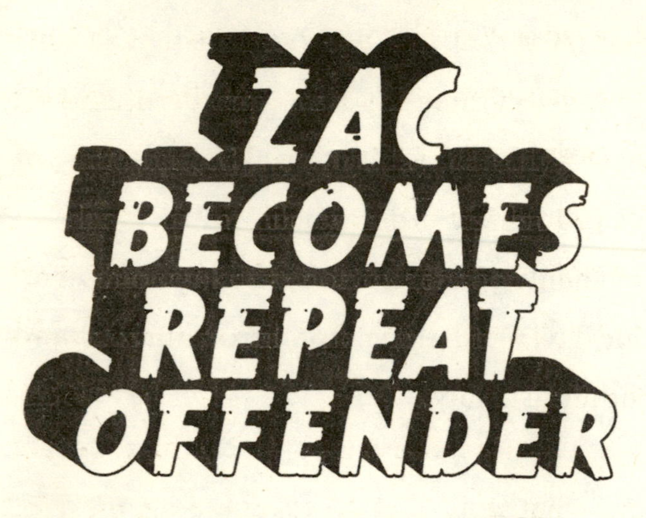

Chapter 11: Zac Becomes Repeat Offender

3 MONTHS AGO

You may be wondering what it is like to be able to turn back time by thirty seconds. In all honesty, it's very hard to describe. It's a bit like déjà vu, only you know it *isn't* déjà vu. You know you have been there before,

and that you have to go there again, a bit like your gran's house. The fact is, it's just one of those things you have to experience in order to fully understand it.

You may be wondering what it is like to be able to turn back time by thirty seconds. In all honesty, it's very hard to describe. It's a bit like déjà vu, only you know it *isn't* déjà vu. You know you have been there before, and that you have to go there again, a bit like your gran's house. The fact is, it's just one of those things you have to experience in order to fully understand it. (See?)

It was a feeling, however, that Zachary Woodward-Lambert had to get used to once he discovered his superpower. None of the girls or boys at school would go near Zac after his outburst, especially not the girl who had tried to be kind to him.

That is, until it occurred to him, that with his newly discovered power, he could win any game he wanted. He joined in the football game and was quickly put in goal, where he made save after spectacular save by rewinding time each time he missed the ball.

'Well played today, you were great!' said Jasper patting him on the back. He had finally been noticed by the coolest kid in school.

And it didn't stop there, every lesson was an opportunity to gain more respect. Now

Zac could do all the things that made Jasper so popular – being good at sport, acting confident and cracking hilarious jokes.

If Jasper said something funny in class, Zac would simply turn back time and say it himself first. Pretty soon he was just as popular as Jasper, and the two of them became best friends.

And before long, Zac received an invitation to the most enviable hang out of all – Jasper's treehouse.

'Honestly, Jasper, this place is amazing, I wish I had a treehouse like this.'

'It's OK, I guess, although my cat Waffles gets stuck up here all the time, which is really annoying.'

'Cool name. So how do you get her down?'

'With great difficulty. I wish superheroes would help out every once in a while. I mean, how much effort is it for them to fly up here and get her down?'

'Not much, I expect.'

'Exactly, whereas I have to climb up myself and risk my life.'

'Yeah, they should definitely lend a hand,' said Zac, secretly not convinced that saving cats from trees was a good use of a superhero's time.

'So, what power would you have if you were a superhero?' asked Jasper, excitedly crossing his arms.

'I … uh …'

'Look, it's easy, take me, for instance, I would want to fly and be invisible,' said Jasper, who seemed quite proud of his answer and was now pretending to fly around the treehouse.

'Isn't that two powers?' asked Zac.

'Well, yeah, but Millie Monday can fly *and* shoot lasers from her eyes. That's two powers. She's so cool.

'Come on, what would *you* want to be able to do?'

'I ... uh ... I would like to be able to turn back time.'

'YES!' said Jasper, jumping to his feet and clapping his hands. 'Bravo, Woodward-Lambert, bravo. I hadn't even considered that. Think of all the things you could do!'

'Well, actually, I can turn back time for real,' said Zac before he could stop himself.

He turned the dial on his watch. It was instinct, to protect himself, he hadn't even seen Jasper's reaction. He composed himself and let it all play out again ...

This time Zac took a deep breath and then spoke.

'Well, actually, I can turn back time for real,' said Zac. He physically had to restrain his arm from turning the dial on his watch. He felt completely exposed. After thirty seconds there would be no turning back and the clock was ticking ...

'Ha, very funny!'

'No, really, I can.'

Jasper looked at him and raised one eyebrow. He seemed to think this was one of Zac's classic jokes, which he had become renowned for recently.

'OK, prove it.'

'How can I prove it?'

'Turn back time.'

'I can only turn it back thirty seconds.'

'That is still very cool. OK, turn it back thirty seconds.'

'But you won't know, I mean, for you it will be just the beginning of this conversation again. Oh wait, I've got it. You think of yourself as a pretty good footballer, right?'

'Best in the school,' said Jasper with a smile.

'So, if I gave you thirty seconds to take as many shots at me as possible, you would

score at least one goal, wouldn't you?'

'Of course! More like ten. I mean, you're good in goal, but no one is *that* good.'

'No, I'm not that good, but as I can turn back time, I know exactly where you will hit the ball. It's like a constant do-over.'

'So what would be thirty seconds for me ...' said Jasper, starting to understand.

'Could be hours for me, until I save every shot.'

★

It took Zac almost eight hours to save every shot. He was exhausted. By the end, though, it had worked. Jasper was convinced.

'That was incredible!' he said, running over to the goal. When he approached he

couldn't believe how sweaty and exhausted Zac was. After all, it had only been thirty seconds for him.

'Oh, man, I'm sorry I ever doubted you. I believe you, Zac. I totally believe you. Let's go inside and get you a drink.'

'Thank you, Jasper.'

'No problem, buddy, and then we can discuss exactly what we are going to do with this extraordinary power of yours.'

In the short time it took to make their way to the back door, enter the kitchen and drink a glass of orange squash, Jasper had already come up with a plan. A plan that would make the world finally stand up

and take even more notice of Jasper Loxton than they already did.

'So what are you going to do with your awesome superpower, Zac?' asked Jasper, pouring another glass of water and visibly shaking in anticipation.

'I ... well, I haven't really thought about it.'

'Look, you have to consider the bigger picture. You know, what side of the fence do you fall?'

'What fence?' Zac was very confused.

'Duh! Are you going to be a superhero or a supervillain?'

'What if I don't want to be either? What if I just want to have a normal life?'

'DON'T SIT ON THE FENCE, WOODWARD-LAMBERT,' said Jasper, finding his inner Terrifying Suzanne and banging his fists on the table. 'I'm sorry,' he said, composing himself. 'You know, I wish I could turn back time to stop that little outburst but I can't. You could, though – don't you see how precious that is? And to just let that go by ...'

'Without helping people ... I know, it's not right. Maybe I want to be a superhero.'

'Without helping *yourself*, you mean,' said Jasper. 'Tell me, what have superheroes ever done for you?'

'Well, they save the world every day, and I'm in the world, so I guess they have saved me,' Zac said, sipping his orange squash through a straw.

'Interesting, but has your life *improved* since they saved the world?'

'Um ...'

'They save the world and for you that is "um". That tells you everything you need to know. Think about what you did with your powers at school. You used them on *yourself*. Tell me, has your life improved?'

'It has.'

'Yes, of course your life has improved – for starters, I'm now in it, giving you all this advice.'

'I really do appreciate it, Jasper.'

'Look, the word "supervillain" sounds

like a bad thing, but really all they are doing is looking after themselves. Is that such a bad thing?' said Jasper, looking directly into Zac's eyes.

'No ... I guess not.'

'Isn't that *exactly* what you did at school?'

'Yeah, I guess ...'

'Then I guess we know which side of the fence you are sitting already ...'

'Thanks, Jasper. You're a good friend. I'm glad I told you.'

'I'm glad too, Zac. You made the right decision.'

After another glass of squash and a plate of waffles (half of which, not surprisingly, were waffled down by Waffles the cat) the boys returned to the treehouse where they spent all night discussing what Zac could do to really make a name for himself.

It turned out that Zac didn't know a whole lot about supervillains. All the stories that came to mind were about superheroes. But Jasper enjoyed telling Zac all about his favourite supervillain – The Legend of Bellyfoot ...

THE LEGEND OF BELLYFOOT

ATM
FREE
CASH
Penguin
pizza!
BOGOHP!

ATM

ATM
FREE
CASH
Penguin
pizza
BOGOHP

'That's what I always liked about Bellyfoot, he could take any normal situation and find a way that his power could make it better for him,' said Jasper.

'Why is he called Bellyfoot?'

'When he found out he could turn into a snake, he didn't want a boring name like "Snake Boy" or "Kid Snake" so he came up with Bellyfoot. You know, because snakes crawl on their belly, so it's both a belly and a foot.'

'I guess that makes sense,' said Zac, not in the slightest bit convinced that it made any sense at all.

'He took a pretty simple power, and used it far beyond what anyone could imagine.

He has made his life a thousand times better. But that's nothing compared to what you could do. You, Zac, you could do anything you wanted. You could take over the world! Look, maybe we just need to get out there, you know? Get that power of yours working,' said Jasper.

'You think I'm ready?' said Zac rather nervously.

'Nah, not really. But you don't need to be ready. You can rewind time until you are,' said Jasper touching the side of his nose.

'I don't know the first thing about taking over the world.'

'Then let's start with a small crime, something challenging that will help get you the reputation as a supervillain not to be messed with. A little bank robbery should do the trick.'

Zac had just taken a large gulp of squash and it came flying out of his mouth in a wet mist.

'I can't do that,' said Zac. 'It took me eight hours to save ten penalties from you earlier, how long will it take to break into a vault, defeat a bunch of superheroes and escape?' asked Zac, curling up into a ball in the corner of the treehouse. He was terrified at the thought of taking on such a huge task. And worried about stealing people's hard-earned money.

'I have no idea, but I can't wait to find out,' said Jasper with a smile.

Chapter 12: The Iguana Cloakroom Service

03:45pm

Dylan practically skipped back to his office with a huge smile on his face. He was the head of the CITD (whatever that meant) at POOP (whatever that meant) and he couldn't wait to get to work. It wasn't until he reached his office door that a rather important question popped into his mind. 'Wait, did he tell me who was in this new team I'm heading up?' he asked.

'Uh ...' said Paul, playing over the conversation in his head. 'I don't think he did. You might get to choose them, how great would that be?'

Dylan was daydreaming about all the cool superheroes he could choose for his team, but as soon as he turned the corner, he was greeted by a long line of people that stretched all the way down to his office.

'Leader of the CITD, trying to make it back to my office, mind out please,' Dylan shouted at the superheroes. *This had better not be a queue to collect coats*, he thought to himself.

In some ways it was worse. Smelly Paul was sitting on the chair, with a little box full of coins, while Red-Eye Paul was hanging from the hook on the door, taking a cape from the superhero at the front of the queue and dropping it, to Dylan's horror, onto the floor. (Dylan knew how precious superheroes were about their capes.) Then the cape was launched up into the air, landing perfectly on a hook at the far end of the room.

The superhero who had given over the cape smiled enthusiastically and dropped a coin on Smelly Paul's tail, who flicked it high into the air before it landed in a bucket with a clang.

'What is going on?' shouted Dylan.

'Oh, hey, Dylan. What do you think of our little business, The Iguana Cloakroom Service?' said Smelly Paul.

'We thought if we have to hang coats all day, we might as well make a little money,' said Red-Eye Paul, taking a coat from another superhero.

'That's lovely, guys, but it won't work,' said Dylan grabbing the coat from Red-Eye and shoving it back into the hand of the superhero who had given it to him. 'This is now the office of the CITD, so kindly take your coat and leave. ALL OF YOU!' shouted Dylan, before slamming the door.

'Don't be a party pooper, we've been getting on famously, haven't we Paula?' Chris said.

Dylan picked Pauline up before she could sink her teeth into his foot.

'Anyway, good news, Ron Strongman has given me a promotion,' Dylan said, sitting down on the chair, feeling incredibly important. 'I don't wish to boast, but I'm the head of the CITD,' he said, full of confidence, hoping they wouldn't feel the need to ask exactly what that stood for (you know, like he hadn't).

'What *exactly* does that stand for?' asked Smelly Paul.

'Yeah, I have no idea and I'm quite happy

to admit that,' added Pauline.

'I ... uh ...' Dylan hadn't even tried to spell it out in his head. He desperately tried to make something up on the spot.

'C-c-c ... cri ... criiiime ... crime, that's the first word.'

'You sure?' asked Red-Eye sarcastically.

'Yep. Crime ... Iiiin ... T-own ... Crime in Town. Da–Du–Dow ... Down! CRIME IN TOWN DOWN,' said Dylan with pure relief.

'So you are the head of Crime In Town Down?' asked Smelly Paul, genuinely confused.

'Shouldn't that be Crime In *Down* Town?' said Pauline. It was a good point. That would have made more sense.

'Oh, I get it, your job is to bring the crime in town … down. That's awesome, man, congratulations!' said Red-Eye running up Dylan's shoulder and giving his other hand a high five.

'Just tell them the truth. You have no idea what it stands for, and you were too scared to ask Ron Strongman,' said Paul.

'I'll find out soon enough, I'm sure.'

At this point, Fifi and Iffi arrived. They stared blankly at Dylan for thirty seconds holding out their hands. It took him a little while to realise they had most likely just asked for their coats back.

Suddenly, Dylan felt a strange vibration in

Click!!

his ear. It was the first time he had received a call on his inner ear piece. 'Calling the head of the CITD, can you hear me?'

'Loud and clear, this is Iguana Boy, head of the CITD at your service.'

'Ah ... yes, yes of course, Iguana Boy ... *that's who I put in charge* ... Ron Strongman calling from POOP HQ here, got an urgent call for you. No time to waste, kid. I will send the details over to you now.'

'Absolutely. My team and I won't let you down Mr Strongman, sir,' said Dylan, forming a salute.

'Actually, sir, I do have one quick question for you. Exactly who else is in my team?'

'Your team?' said Ron Strongman, sounding confused.

'Yes, my team. You put me in charge of a department, so I presume I have a team at my disposal?'

'Yes, yes, quite right. Tell me, who is in that office of yours right now?'

'Uh, right now? Well, I share an office with VentriloChris and Terrifying Suzanne, and right now the Telepathy Twins are here with me,' said Dylan, hoping to direct the conversation AWAY from the most annoying superheroes in the world.

'Ah yes, brilliant. They will do.'

'Do what, sir?'

'Exactly, yes!' said Ron ignoring the question entirely. 'You all have my permission to leave the building on this important mission. We are on lockdown after all.'

'Thank you, sir' said Dylan, touching the side of his ear to end the call. 'Right, we have our very first mission, you guys ready?' said Dylan.

'Sure thing!' said Red-Eye, climbing into Dylan's rucksack.

'Can't wait,' added Pauline joining him.

'Wait, who were the other members of your team?' asked Paul.

Iffi and Fifi both had a beep on their phones at the same time. They took them out and looked up at Dylan. He wasn't sure what they said, but they smiled.

'Well, Iffi and Fifi are in. I'll tell you about the others on the way,' said Dylan.

MISSION IMPOSSIBLE

05:30pm

The CITD's first mission was at a very large house in the nice part of town. Dylan arrived, with his iguanas and the Telepathy Twins, to find VentriloChris and Terrifying Suzanne were already waiting on the drive

with a young fair-haired boy.

'Well, if it isn't Mr Head of the CITD himself!' said VentriloChris excitedly, waving as Dylan walked up the drive. 'Congratulations again on the promo, buddy, truly deserved.' He was still quite a distance away from Dylan but that didn't stop him from speaking to him enthusiastically.

'IT'S HIS FIRST DAY, HOW DOES HE DESERVE A PROMOTION, YOU FOOL?' shouted Terrifying Suzanne. It was a good point. Dylan thought that if she didn't shout so much, perhaps Terrifying Suzanne could be a real asset.

'OK, guys, good to see you, even you, Terrifying Suzanne,' said Dylan trying to cut the tension. She stared at him and he could have sworn she let out the slightest growl. 'OK, you didn't find that funny, consider it noted.'

'Hello, sir, my name is Iguana Boy, how can we help you this evening?' he asked the fair-haired boy.

'Hi, I'm Jasper. You're rather late. I will decide whether or not to lodge a formal complaint with Superhero HQ,' he said. 'Anyway, my cat is stuck in that tree, stupid thing. Be quick about getting her down, I have places I need to be tonight,' he snapped, clearly growing frustrated.

'Wait, your *cat* is stuck in a tree? You know that wasting a superhero's time is considered to be a crime?' said Dylan.

'Don't lecture me, I saw it on the news earlier that you guys were helping cats down from trees. Set up a whole department to tackle the issue head on, apparently.'

Dylan's heart sank and the words hit him like a wave against jagged rocks in a tropical storm.

'CITD ... Cats In Trees Department,' he muttered, piecing it all together.

'It's about time you actually did something useful like this. I'm sure it's just a publicity stunt because Repeat Offender is making you all look like fools, but I don't really care. And if that is the reason, I hope you never catch him. Waffles gets stuck up that tree at least twice a week.'

'Hey,' said Dylan,

'Repeat Offender is a supervillain and he is causing havoc across London. We will stop him, I guarantee it.'

'*You* are going to stop him? You and who's army, this bunch of misfits behind you? How exactly are you going to stop a supervillain who can turn back time by thirty seconds?' said Jasper, laughing hysterically. 'He will always be one step ahead of you. Now get my cat down from that tree.'

Jasper laughed all the way back to the house and when he was inside, Dylan turned to face his team.

'Did you hear that?' he said, lowering his voice.

'Yeah I heard him all right' said Iffi.

'Thinks we are a piece of poop on his shoes.'

'Speaking of which, have you heard the Superhero Collective is now called POOP?' said VentriloChris.

'Who cares about that?' said Dylan, desperate to get back to the matter at hand, only his curiosity got the better of him. 'Actually, that has been bugging me, anyone even know what it stands for?'

'It stands for the Protection Organisation for Ordinary People. POOP for short,' said VentriloChris.

'Ah, I see. Well, when you spell it out like that, it's still a really stupid name,' said Paul.

'That is an awful name. Makes no sense at all,' said Dylan.

'Terrible,' said Fifi.

'Terrib ... bbbbad,' said Iffi, trying to be different.

'I like it,' said VentriloChris.

'I HATE POOP!' shouted Terrifying Suzanne. (Dylan wasn't entirely sure she was talking about the same thing as the rest of them.)

'Right, let's get to work,' said VentriloChris, walking towards the tree.

'Wait, wait, wait,' said Dylan, suddenly remembering what he had heard. 'That kid, do you remember what he said about Repeat Offender?' Everyone looked blankly at him. 'He said that Repeat Offender could turn back time by thirty seconds.'

'OK ...' said VentriloChris.

'Don't you remember what Ron Strongman said in the briefing earlier? He said no one knows how Repeat Offender has been breaking into banks. No one knows what his superpower is.'

'Ah, man, yeah that would be really useful info to help stop him, isn't that right?' said VentriloChris.

'That kid just told us! He was so busy trying to show he was better than us, he accidentally let it slip.'

'But what makes you think he even knows?' asked Fifi.

'If he didn't know, why even say it? Besides, my gut is saying there is something more to that kid. Who knows, it might even be him.'

'Let's go get him right now then!' said Iffi. Fifi held her back.

'No, we don't want to arouse suspicion. The best thing we can do is rescue Waffles.'

'You still want to rescue this kid's cat? He was pretty rude, not to mention a potential supervillain,' said VentriloChris.

'Innocent until proven guilty, VentriloChris. Besides, we have been given a job by Ron Strongman and it is our sworn duty as members of the Superhero Collective to carry it out.'

'You mean POOP,' said Paul, trying to hold back laughter. Dylan ignored him.

'It's our sworn duty to carry out the

mission assigned to us. Let's go and save that cat.'

The theory goes that rescuing a cat from a very tall tree is a fairly simple task for a superhero. If the average ordinary person tried to do it, well, they would risk hurting themselves and probably graze their knees on the rough bark. A superhero, however, could fly on up there, and bring themselves and the cat safely back to earth. Right?

Wrong.

The flightless superheroes stood at the bottom of the tree looking up at the cat, which was perched on the tip of a branch.

'I'VE DONE THIS BEFORE ...' said Terrifying Suzanne before screaming at the top of her voice, 'GET DOWN FROM THAT TREE, YOU STUPID CAT!'

The cat didn't move. It didn't even flinch.

'OK, any other ideas?' said Dylan.

'I mean, I guess we could try, you know … climbing?' said VentriloChris.

'Have you seen the height of that tree?' said Iffi.

'And how delicate our nails are?' said Fifi. 'Which have just been manicured.'

'Not you, obviously,' said VentriloChris moving slowly backwards. 'I mean, maybe Dylan could go up there, or even one of his iguanas, I bet they are great climbers.'

'I guess they are fairly decent climbers.' Dylan looked over at his iguana friends. They didn't look too impressed. If VentriloChris hadn't come up with the idea perhaps they would have entertained it, but it didn't look like they were going to do anything he suggested.

'I'll do it, I will climb the stupid tree.' Dylan took off his rucksack and began to climb. The bark was really rough and thick. He grazed his knees before he was even at the first branch. 'This is going to be painful.'

After fifteen minutes and nearly as many marks on his arms and legs, he reached the branch where the cat was sitting. It was at this point that Paul, who had been looking at him from the ground, ran up the tree and joined Dylan on the branch. It took him fifteen seconds.

'Hey, dude, how's it going?'

Dylan was too petrified, and concentrating too hard on not falling, to reply.

He began to head out and the branch wobbled. 'There is no way I can go out there, it's too thin. We will both come falling down.'

'Don't worry about that, cats land on their feet!' said VentriloChris rather unhelpfully.

'HE WASN'T WORRIED ABOUT THE CAT, YOU FOOL!'

'Be careful, Dylan!' shouted Pauline, genuinely concerned.

'Paul, perhaps now you are up here you would go out and get Waffles?'

'Sorry, man, I just came up here to watch.

Terrible view from down there, and I wanted a front-row seat to you making a fool of yourself!'

'Paul! Be nice,' said Pauline sternly.

Paul straightened up and began to murmur. 'Uhhh ... I mean ... you're the real superhero, and I wouldn't want to take away the glory from your FIRST official mission. You can do it, Iguana Boy!' Paul started jumping up and down, clapping in excitement, making the branch sway violently.

'Oh. Sorry, buddy.' He stopped and Dylan regained his composure. 'Ooh, wait. I have an idea,' said Paul. Why doesn't VentriloChris make the noise of a bird right next to the cat's ear, and then lead her across the

branch to us?'

'That's an excellent idea! He is good at making irritating noises. VentriloChris, make the noise of a bird, and get Waffles to follow it across the branch towards me.'

'Uh ... sure,' said VentriloChris, before letting out a gentle chirp. At first Waffles began swatting around her ears, thinking the bird was right next to her. This caused the branch to sway, almost knocking Dylan off balance and out of the tree again. Both regained their balance and, slowly but surely, Waffles began to make her way across the branch towards Dylan.

'Here, kitty, kitty, kitty, kitty,' cooed Dylan, slowly moving his finger like a snake-charmer's snake. Waffles was close enough to grab, but Dylan thought if he went for it too soon and missed, she would almost certainly head back out onto the branch.

He hesitated and then, with his legs wrapped around the branch and his feet interlocked, he grabbed Waffles by the belly. Waffles did not like being grabbed by the belly.

Waffles let out a screech and swiped her right claw in the direction of Dylan's face. He managed to put his arm up just in time. He felt her jagged nails claw the length of his forearm and let out a howl, as Waffles skipped past him and casually jumped through the window of the treehouse, opened the treehouse door and pirouetted down from the tree.

'See, they always land on their feet,' said VentriloChris as Waffles trotted gently back towards the house. Dylan, exhausted, collapsed on the branch in a heap.

'Right, well, a successful first mission,' said Dylan, ten minutes later, after he had climbed down from the tree. 'Good job, everyone, let's head back to Superhero HQ and report back to Ron Strongman.'

The following week went by incredibly slowly. There hadn't been a single incident from Repeat Offender since he had walked away with the princely sum of five pounds from the Greater London Bank the week before. A wave of frustration swept across Superhero HQ (or should that be POOP

HQ?) Dylan had heard it was the longest amount of time they had ever been on lockdown and that Ron Strongman was losing his mind.

With every passing day the reputation of POOP was, well, going down the toilet. Which is not a place POOP was happy to be. With it came an increased workload for Dylan and the rest of the CITD team. They were beginning to get to know each other very well.

A week later ...

01:00pm

02:30pm
GO GET THE KITTY DOWN, DOGGY!
NOOO!
GO GET THEM DOWN, GOAT!
UGH! GO GET THEM DOWN, HORSE!
SNAP!

YAY!

04:00pm

'Uh ... guys,' said Dylan, looking up at the iguanas sitting in the tree. 'What are you doing?'

Dylan noticed that the tree was shaking, though there was no wind. It was a beautiful summer's day. It was his iguana pals – they were shaking in fear.

'Oh, I see,' said Dylan, understanding that his pals were too scared to climb back down in the direction of Terrifying Suzanne's belly-booming shout. 'How about we get some pizza?'

'PIZZA?' said Paul snapping out of his trance.

'Great idea, Dylan,' said Smelly Paul.

'Yeah, you're my favourite horse!' said Red-Eye.

‘For the hundredth time, he’s a human!’ said Pauline.

‘Same thing,’ said Red-Eye, shrugging his shoulders.

When they had made their way down from the tree, Dylan could see that the iguanas looked as tired as he felt. He decided a little break would do them all good. He knew just the place to take them.

‘Let’s head over to I Dream of Pizza,’ said Dylan.

The iguanas jumped for joy and began high-fiving each other. This was their FAVOURITE pizza takeaway. It was situated next door to a little shop called Pets Behaving Badly, which just so happened to be where they had grown up. The smell of the pizza used to drift through the air vents and fill their cage and their lungs with cheesy goodness. It was where they had first fallen in love with pizza.

'YES!' said Paul, punching the air. 'I dream of I Dream of Pizza all the time.'

'Me too. Hey, maybe we can drop in on the owner of Pets Behaving Badly and that stupid dog of his. Bet it will give him a real scare seeing us again!' said Smelly Paul.

'That *isn't* the sort of behaviour you would expect from a superhero,' said Dylan. Smelly Paul apologised and they made their way over to I Dream of Pizza.

Dylan ordered two extra-large triple-cheese pizzas with extra cheese. They had a great time, all the while filling their stomachs with incredible-tasting pizza. Dylan told his favourite jokes, Smelly Paul made fart noises (it was hard to tell if they were JUST noises as the smell was always pretty bad), Paul did impressions of everyone (his impression of Dylan was particularly well received), Pauline told the story of the time she had hit VentriloChris, and Crazy Red-Eye Paul ran head-first into the wall. It was a great evening, and for a short while, Dylan forgot all about the stresses of running the CITD.

They left the restaurant still laughing, and came to a stop outside Pets Behaving Badly.

'The place it all began,' said Dylan, reminiscing.

'You know it would be nice to drop in, say hello to a few of our old friends,' said Paul, giving Dylan's ear a little nudge with his tail.

'If you promise NOT to scare the poor shopkeeper.'

'We promise,' said Pauline, seemingly speaking on behalf of the group. Perhaps Dylan should have asked them all to answer individually, because as soon as they entered, Smelly Paul leapt from Dylan's shoulder and landed on the magazine the shopkeeper was reading.

The magazine flew from his hands, and the shopkeeper looked down to see one of the scariest, most badly behaved animals he had ever had the displeasure of knowing.

'AAAARRGHHHH!' he screeched.

'WHHHOOOOOOOFFFFFF,' barked the dog, which is dog-speak for "AAAARRGHHHH!"

Dylan ran over and picked Smelly Paul up and placed him back on his shoulder.

'I'm not taking them back. You couldn't pay me to have them back in here,' said the shopkeeper, absolutely petrified.

'Sorry about that. I've actually spent a great deal of time with these iguanas and they are MUCH better behaved now. I promise.'

'I don't care. No refunds.'

'No, you misunderstand, I'm not here to

give them back. I want to keep them.'

'Good riddance,' said the shopkeeper, breathing a huge sigh of relief. The dog was shaking in the corner, his paw covering his eyes. 'Wait ... then why are you here? Surely you didn't come in just to scare me?'

Smelly Paul smiled. It would appear that had been the reason, although Dylan had been assured it wasn't. Dylan spoke without thinking.

'Of course not. I'm looking to buy another animal from you.'

'If I recall you didn't actually buy those wretched iguanas.'

'Oh, I'm sorry, would you prefer to have them back?' Dylan held Smelly Paul out in front of him. The shopkeeper sprang backwards, hitting his head on a shelf.

'No, no ... what are you looking for?'

That was a good question. Dylan had no idea. In fact, he really didn't want the responsibility of another animal, and then it hit him. Literally.

'OUCH!' said Dylan hopping on one leg and bending down to hold the other. Something had savagely struck him. He looked down just in time to see a savage blur of claws and fangs.

'He got out again! How does he do it?' said the shopkeeper,

who was hastily putting on an all-in-one boiler suit and some thick gloves.

'What was that?' said Dylan, his leg really beginning to sting.

'That was Keith. He is pretty volatile, keeps escaping from his cage in the restricted section. Say, you weren't looking to buy a cat, were you?'

'KEITH?' said Paul, gripping Dylan's shoulder tightly.

'A friend of yours?'

'No. He isn't the friendly type. Doesn't mix well with others ...'

Dylan heard a vicious hiss from behind him, and once more felt a savage swipe, this time at his other leg.

Keith was moving so quickly it was hard to keep up.

'He's a little bit scratchy, but if you have the right equipment he really can be quite cute,' said the shopkeeper. Dylan noticed that the shopkeeper was wearing an American football helmet in addition to the suit and gloves. He was holding a hockey stick in one hand, and a large air horn in the other.

'Most importantly, he doesn't like loud noises.' The shopkeeper pressed the air horn, which made an almighty trumpet sound. Dylan and the iguanas covered their ears as they watched Keith shoot up the shelves behind the shopkeeper before cowering on the top shelf.

'I actually found Keith one day when I was driving around town,' said the shopkeeper, taking off his helmet. He was standing in the middle of the road looking lost and I beeped my horn. He shot straight up the nearest and tallest tree.'

A lightbulb flashed above Dylan's head. The bulb was old and needed replacing, but it just so happened that Dylan had a FANTASTIC idea at the exact same time.

'We'll take him!' said Dylan.

The iguanas looked on in shock. It was the first time he had ever seen them speechless. Dylan savoured the moment.

'Why would you want a vicious, horrible cat?' asked Pauline, utterly perplexed.

'The CITD has a very clear purpose, which as superheroes, we must uphold,' said Dylan.

'What's that exactly?' asked Red-Eye.

'To save cats from trees.'

'Oh yeah, I remember now.'

'Of course, should we be called out to save a cat from a tree and another crime was happening in the vicinity of that tree, and we just so happened to witness it ... we couldn't stand idly by ...'

'What are you saying?' asked Paul.

'I'm saying we have a duty as superheroes to help others, and if we saw someone in need whilst out on CITD business, we would help them.'

'That's brilliant,' said Pauline, a smile beaming from ear to ear. 'Such a clever idea.'

Red-Eye began clapping, causing the other iguanas to cheer. 'Fantastic! I love it. If we kidnap all the troublesome cats, they won't get stuck in trees and we can be redeployed to more important jobs.'

'I don't think that's what he is planning,' said Pauline. 'Correct me if I'm wrong, but I'm thinking Keith here may find his way up a tree or two in the near future.'

'Go on,' said Dylan, waving his finger in a circling motion for her to continue.

'Perhaps outside a bank ...'

'Almost there ...'

'A bank that may be getting burgled ...'

'And who might that burglar be?'

'KEITH!' shouted Red-Eye standing up on Dylan's shoulder and pointing at the cat. 'Because Keith is a CAT-BURGLAR! That's a thing, right?'

'I see where you're going with this, but

I think it may be Repeat Offender who is robbing the bank,' said Pauline.

'Bingo! Next time he robs a bank, all we need to do is get Keith here up the nearest tree, which by the looks of things, won't be too hard. Then we have a reason to be there,' said Dylan.

'And we couldn't stand idly by,' added Pauline.

★

Coaxing Keith down from the shelf was not easy. By the time they had managed to get him down and into a carry cage, they were scratched and exhausted.

'So, how much do you want for him?' asked Dylan?

'You want KEITH?' said the shopkeeper, utterly perplexed. 'Not sure what is wrong with you, kid, first those wretched iguanas and now ... take him. Please... just take him.'

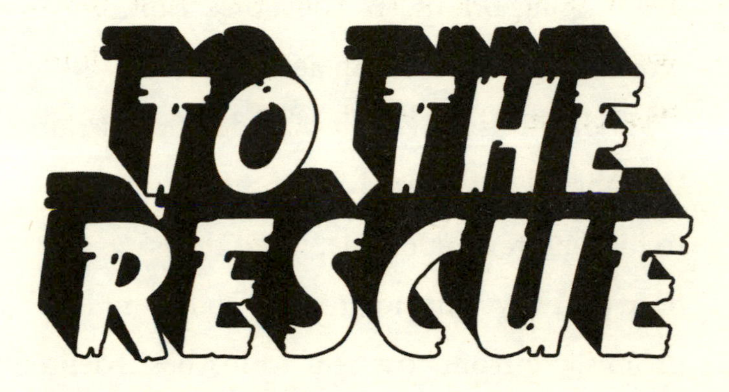

05:45pm

Zac, aka Repeat Offender, had been standing outside the Greater Royal London bank for almost fifteen minutes now, and the guard outside the front door was beginning to get

suspicious. It was obvious, he kept pretending to tie his shoe lace when it was already done up, looking briefly in Zac's direction as he went down and back up again.

He didn't usually wait outside, he just ran straight in and waited for the first problem to hit him, rewound time, fixed the issue and he was away. But not today. Today he had promised a front-row seat to his best friend who was desperate to see him in action.

Jasper had of course followed the news and seen the CCTV footage, but he wanted to witness it in person. He had promised to meet him at 5.30 p.m. outside the bank, but he was late.

'Let's do this!' said Jasper, jumping onto

Zac's back from behind him. 'Ha! I can't believe I surprised you. You will need to be much more aware of your surroundings in there,' said Jasper pointing at the bank. Zac thought about rewinding time and moving out of the way, but he was so distracted by what Jasper was wearing, he completely forgot.

'What are you wearing?' said Zac, pushing his friend down to the ground to try and avoid the eye of the security guard.

'What, this?' said Jasper, pulling at his long-sleeved black top. 'I guess it's a little tight, must have shrunk in the wash.'

'Not just the top, the whole outfit,' said Zac. 'Wait, are those oven gloves?'

GR
LO
ROY
BA
RO

‘These things? Yeah, probably, I did find them in the kitchen. Last-minute decision as I left the house, don’t want to be leaving any prints at the scene,’ said Jasper, clapping his hands. There was clearly some leftover flour on the gloves, which shot up Jasper’s nose causing him to have a coughing fit.

‘You’re drawing attention to us! Besides, you don’t need to worry about leaving fingerprints as you aren’t going to touch anything. You promised not to get involved, remember?’

‘I actually promised not to *interfere*, but don’t worry, I won’t get in the way,’ said Jasper with a big smile. ‘Come on, buddy, let’s do this!’

Zac sighed, he was beginning to regret inviting Jasper along, but he found it very hard to say no to him. 'OK, but just ... stay out of the way. And take that stupid balaclava off.'

'Deal,' said Jasper, although he made no move to remove the piece of headwear ... or the oven gloves.

They made their way across the road, and no sooner had Zac walked past the guard he felt a hand on his shoulder.

'Not so fast, mister,' said the security guard. He turned Zac around and his eyes grew wider. 'Wait a second, you're ... you're that Repeat Offender! SOUND THE ALARM!'

'This is going to be a long day,' said Zac,

looking down at his watch for the first of many times.

YOU'RE ...
YOU'RE THAT REPEAT OFFENDER! SOUND THE ALARM!
AH! THIS IS SO FRUSTRATING!
RO
THAT WAS INCREDIBLE! HOW MANY ATTEMPTS DID THAT TAKE?
JUST THE ONE ...
BANK

05:50pm

Back around the corner again ...

Dylan was standing outside Pets Behaving Badly with the Pauls, Pauline and Keith when he heard a faint crackling message in his earpiece. There was no doubt the voice belonged to Ron Strongman.

'Reported sighting of Repeat Offender at the Great London Bank. Or was it the Royal London Bank? No ... no ... The Greater Royal London Bank ... Why do all the banks sound exactly the same? Just ... STOP HIM!'

'It's Repeat Offender ... robbing a bank right now!' said Dylan to his iguanas, breathing heavily.

'Oh, wow, which one?' said Pauline.

'Uh, honestly I'm not sure. The Great Royal London Bank of Greater London maybe. Ron Strongman is right, they really need to come up with some different names.'

'We passed a bank on our way here. It was just around the corner. If we are going to help, we need to get Keith up a nearby tree fast,' said Paul.

'We had just better hope it's the right bank,' said Smelly Paul.

And that is when they heard the bank alarm. It was just around the corner.

'Phew!' said Dylan, he put his finger to his ear and spoke.

'Calling all CITD members. I have come across a cat stuck up a tree. I'm going to need ALL of your help immediately.'

CATS AND BURGLARS

As Dylan approached the street corner, the alarm grew even louder. He slowed down briefly as he took the bend and came to a complete stop. The street was empty. They had done it, they had beaten the police and, more importantly, any superhero to the scene of the crime. Finally, a bit of luck.

'Great, we are first here, that means—'

'I'm way ahead of you,' said Red-Eye, opening up the door to Keith's cage.

'What are you doing?' said Dylan, reaching for the cage, but it was too late, Keith had already shot up the nearest tree. 'Great, now we are going to have to get him down.'

'Wasn't that the point?' said Red-Eye, totally confused.

'We could have pretended we had already saved him. Now we will actually have to RESCUE that awful cat.'

'Oh yeah, that's a pretty clever idea. Bet you wish you had told me beforehand.'

'Never mind, let's get into the bank and

worry about the cat after,' said Dylan, as his brother and sister appeared at the street corner, arguing as they ran.

'I don't care if it's a Monday, I'm going to take Repeat Offender down,' said Arctic Thunder for what didn't appear to be the first time.

'BUT IT'S A MONDAY!' screamed Millie Monday hysterically. 'That's my day!'

Arctic Thunder was just about to continue the argument when he noticed his little brother.

'What do we have here then?' asked Arctic Thunder, just as the rest of the CITD turned up. 'Ah, I see,' said Arctic Thunder, pointing up at Keith. He and Millie Monday both laughed. 'You know that was MY idea, the whole CITD thing,' he said.

'Wait, what?'

'I suggested to Ron he gave the job of saving POOP's reputation to you and that the best way to do it was by rescuing cats in trees!'

'Genius,' said Millie Monday.

Arctic Thunder gave his sister a high five without even looking at her. They landed it perfectly.

'You know what, I don't care,' said Dylan, refusing to let them ruffle his feathers AGAIN. 'You may have set out to annoy me, but it hasn't worked. Instead you helped bring together an incredible superhero team that are going to capture Repeat Offender and SAVE THE WORLD.'

'No, you are going to save that cat, little bro,' said Arctic Thunder.

'We came here to save the cat,' said Dylan, beginning to put his masterplan into action, 'BUT we cannot stand idly by as a supervillain—'

'That is exactly what you will do. Your job is to save cats from trees.'

'But it would take you two seconds to fly up there and bring that cat down, then we could all take on Repeat Offender together,' said VentriloChris, who was now standing by Dylan's side. Arctic Thunder let out a mighty chuckle.

'I don't have time to save cats from trees. Besides, it would also take me two seconds to do this ...' Arctic Thunder grabbed hold of Dylan and flew up into the air. He took Dylan over to where Keith was lying on the branch and, for the briefest of seconds, Dylan thought he was actually going to help him rescue the cat. Instead, he let go of him and dropped Dylan next to Keith, leaving him stranded up the tree.

'Right, enough of this,' said Arctic Thunder, 'I have to go and save the world.' Off he flew into the bank.

'BUT IT'S A MONDAY!' screamed Millie Monday, picking up where their argument had left off.

Millie flew up to the branch and grabbed hold of Dylan. 'Don't tell ANYONE I did this, but I've had enough of Sam thinking he is SO much better because his powers work every day,' she said, picking up the cat too and flying to the ground, before heading into the bank.

Once Dylan was back on the ground, the team got thinking.

'How on earth are we going to stop a supervillain who can turn back time?' asked Iffi.

'Fantastic question,' said Paul, who had asked the same thing himself.

But Dylan completely ignored him. He had noticed a woman sitting on a bench crying, being consoled by a security guard from the bank. Fat lot of good he was doing out here.

'Hello?' said Iffi.

'That's very rude you know, being asked a question and staring blankly into space,' added Fifi.

'Sorry,' said Dylan, still not entirely back in the conversation. 'I was momentarily distracted.' Another lightbulb ... 'THAT'S IT!'

'What is it?' said Paul.

'We are going to have to distract him' said Dylan.

'Distract him? How?' asked Pauline.

'He can rewind time by thirty seconds, right?' said Dylan, clearly thinking out loud. 'All we need to do after catching him is distract him for thirty seconds, because if he rewinds time more than thirty seconds AFTER we have captured him, he won't be able to escape!'

'That's a great plan, but how are we going to distract him for thirty seconds?' said Iffi.

'Look around you,' said Dylan with a smile. 'Have you met the CITD?'

Inside the bank things had been running quite smoothly. Well, that's if you were to ask Jasper how things were going, of course. From his point of view it had looked effortless. A nicely timed mint thrown at a bird kicked it all off, and inside he had witnessed Repeat Offender hide behind all manner of objects and people, avoiding detection with split-second timing.

In actual fact he had been caught well over one hundred times and was feeling exhausted. Despite this, he had managed to make it to the vault, break in and was on his way out when Arctic Thunder flew in.

'Your time is up, Repeat Offender, I suggest you take one last look around at the free world. You know, maybe once we leave the bank, it's a bit dull in here,' he said, releasing a small spatter of rain over the villain. 'Perhaps look at a tree or something, because where you are going ... What I'm trying to say is, you're going to prison,' said

Arctic Thunder.

Millie Monday flew in around this time.

At this point they argued amongst themselves for a few more seconds, allowing Repeat Offender to turn back time. Repeat Offender made his way towards the exit, when he was suddenly grabbed from behind. 'What the ...' said Repeat Offender, looking at the doorway to see a group of superheroes (at least he thought they were superheroes) standing by the entrance.

'DON'T MOVE, YOU FOOL!' shouted Terrifying Suzanne who had grabbed hold of him.

'Look over here.'

'OR here.'

'OR even over there,'

said VentriloChris, sending his voice all over the bank. Repeat Offender looked in each of the directions, completely bamboozled.

'Good job, Terrifying Suzanne,' said Iffi.

'HEY! I was going to say that. STOP READING MY MIND!' screamed Fifi, who then began pulling her sister's hair.

'Your time is up, Repeat Offender,' said Dylan holding Keith above his head. The plan was working perfectly. Repeat Offender looked absolutely CONFUZZLED, just as they had hoped. Dylan glanced at his watch, twenty seconds had passed. They were almost there ...

'Is that a cat?' asked Repeat Offender,

trying to figure out why a superhero would be carrying a cat. 'This is all so ... DISTRACTING!' said Repeat Offender, suddenly snapping out of his trance. 'Did you really think I wouldn't figure out what you were ...' He froze. 'What the ...?'

Paul appeared first, sitting on top of a remote-control car, his tail doing the

steering with the controller. He was wearing sunglasses and was clapping his hands.

Next to appear was Pauline. She was hanging from the bottom of a remote-control helicopter, holding on tightly with her tail, a small controller in her hand. Dylan was just as surprised as Repeat Offender – he had no idea where the remote-control vehicles had come from.

Suddenly, Repeat Offender started to feel sick. 'What is that terrible smell?'

'That would be me,' said Smelly Paul proudly, tapping him on the shoulder with his tail. He had been hiding in Terrifying Suzanne's bag and had climbed on to Repeat Offender's shoulder at the perfect time.

There were just a couple of seconds left. Dylan gave the signal.

'NOW!' he shouted (it was a pretty effective signal).

Crazy Red-Eye Paul jumped out of Dylan's bag, waving his arms around frantically, before putting both feet in front of him and launching himself at Repeat Offender.

'K'POW!' he shouted, before landing *at least* ten feet away from his target, crashing head-first into the ground.

'Ooooh. That looks like it really hurt,' said Dylan. 'Incredibly distracting, though.'

'I ... uh ...' But it was too late. At last Repeat Offender reversed time, but he had already been caught by Terrifying Suzanne and there was simply nothing he could do to break free. 'You win, I surrender,' said Repeat Offender, completely deflated.

'We did it!' shouted Dylan, helping Pauline down from the helicopter. Paul jumped off the car and ran over to help Red-Eye up from the ground. He was a little dazed and confused (it really had been a hard landing).

'Did I get him?' said Red-Eye, who was seeing stars.

'You got him all right. You were all like, K'POW!' said Paul. Red-Eye smiled and let himself fall into his arms.

Arctic Thunder looked over at Terrifying Suzanne holding Repeat Offender, and his brother celebrating.

'NOT AGAIN!' he said, before quickly fleeing the scene, dragging Millie with him. The last time he had been saved by his brother, he tried to take some of the credit. This time he wanted to forget he had ever been there.

'OK, Repeat Offender,' said Dylan, turning to the supervillain. 'Any final words before you're brought to justice?'

'I'm sorry,' said Repeat Offender.

Dylan was shocked. Supervillains didn't usually say anything at all at this point in the proceedings.

'Excuse me?' asked Dylan, checking to see if he had heard correctly.

'I would like to apologise,' Repeat

Offender repeated, bowing his head and closing his eyes. 'I don't expect you to accept my apology, or even believe it's genuine, but nonetheless I want to say it because it's true. I'm sorry. I didn't think what I was doing was hurting anyone, but I see now how naïve I have been.'

'I don't understand. I have never heard a supervillain APOLOGISE before. It makes me wonder, why you did it in the first place,' said Dylan, moving closer to him.

'I ...' Repeat Offender paused. Dylan could almost feel his shame. 'I just wanted people to think I was cool. I never had friends and being able to turn back time made me popular. I wanted the cool boy at school to like me and want to be my friend. I guess I was so busy trying to impress the people around me that I didn't stop to think if what I was doing was right or wrong. I understand now that it was wrong, of course, and I know I am going to go to prison, but please believe me, I'm not a bad person.' As he spoke, a tear fell down his cheek. Dylan didn't need to see him cry. He believed every single word.

'Not a bad person, hey?' said a policeman who had entered towards the end of Repeat Offender's speech. 'I think the bank manager would have something to say about that.'

'I only ever took five pounds from any bank. In fact, the money never even left the bank. I always slipped it into the security guard's pocket on the way out. Actually, that's not true, once I did give it to a guy because his kid was crying and he looked like he could do with an ice cream.'

'What about the other one million, nine hundred and ninety-nine thousand and ninety-five pounds? Would that make you a *bad person?*' said the policeman.

'What?' said Repeat Offender, genuinely surprised.

'I think it's fair to say that would make him a pretty bad person,' said VentriloChris.

'I never stole anything more than a five-pound note. I swear!'

'Tell that to your lawyer, kid, 'cause the

bank manager has informed us there is two million pounds missing, and you're the one who broke into the vault. Come with me.'

'JASPER! It had to be Jasper!' screamed Repeat Offender, suddenly realising he hadn't seen his friend since he entered the vault. 'I never wanted to do any of this, I really only ever wanted to help people, but Jasper convinced me that I should help myself. I feel so foolish. But I want to help you put this right. Find him and you will find the money.'

Terrifying Suzanne handed Repeat Offender over to the police officer, but as she did so, Keith jumped out of Dylan's hands and charged at the policeman. The cat flew through the air and knocked him cleanly off his feet. No one was holding on to Repeat Offender ...

For a moment, no one moved, they simply stared at him. He was free and that meant he could turn back time. However, Dylan was pretty sure he didn't. Instead Repeat Offender simply bent down to pick the cat up.

'I wouldn't do that if I were you,' said Dylan, bracing as he waited for Keith to turn into a vicious blur of claws and fangs once more. Instead, he seemed quite happy and purred gently.

'Lead the way officer. I shan't resist,' said Zac.

'I don't think he stole all the cash, I really don't,' said Dylan.

'Me neither,' said Paul.

'Say, Dylan, do you think I could borrow your cape?' said Pauline out of nowhere.

'Uh ... why would you need my cape?' Superheroes were pretty protective of their capes.

'Just a little cold in here, wouldn't you say?' said Pauline raising her eyebrows knowingly at him. It was clear she was trying to tell him something, but he had absolutely no idea what.

'Are you kidding, it's ROASTING in here!' said Red-Eye.

Dylan bent down and placed his cape over

Pauline. Suddenly the cape was launched high into the air with an almighty flick of Pauline's tail. It rose almost as high as the chandelier as it made its way across the vast room of the bank.

Zac and the police officer stopped in their tracks, distracted by Pauline's skill.

'Surely not,' said Smelly Paul, his mouth agape as he pointed towards a solitary coat stand at the other end of the room. The cape was heading right for it ...

Everyone watched with baited breath, as the cape descended towards the coat stand, only to see it fly clear over it, even making it past the rather large potted plant behind it.

Pauline had missed the coat stand completely.

'HA!' shouted Paul hysterically. 'See, I told you, it was all luck. No skill involved WHATSOEVER.'

'I wasn't aiming at the coat stand,' said Pauline, a smile widening on her face.

All of a sudden, a boy wearing all black and oven gloves came tumbling out from behind the pot with a cape draped over his head. He fell flat on his face, dropping the

huge grey bag he was carrying and spilling bundles of cash to the floor. Dylan couldn't be certain, but it looked to be around two million pounds (well, two million minus a fiver).

'That's him! That's Jasper!' said Zac. Jasper stumbled to his feet.

'You fools,' said Jasper. 'Did you honestly think that wet bag of lettuce Zachary Woodward-Lambert was the BRAINS behind this operation?' he said slapping his thigh and chuckling. He took off his balaclava and turned to face Dylan.

'You! I knew there was something off about you the moment I met you,' said Dylan.

Jasper smiled and flicked his hair. He turned to face Zac and addressed him directly. 'You were given an AWESOME power and what did you choose to do with it? MAKE FRIENDS! "Oh boo hoo, nobody likes me ... please like me!" It's pathetic.' Jasper laughed, pretending to rub tears away from his eyes.

'Why couldn't I have received his power? I would have put it to PROPER use. Not that it matters, I got what I wanted anyway.' He gestured towards the huge bag of cash. 'And with this kind of money I can buy a whole team of supervillains to use as I see fit, and TAKE OVER THE WORLD! And there isn't a damn thing any of you can do to stop me.'

Having performed his rather drawn-out yet elegant supervillain monologue (he really would have made a pretty good supervillain), he ran towards the door.

They didn't have much time before he would get away. Thinking fast, Paul kicked the remote control of the racing car over to VentriloChris and said, 'You know what to do.'

VentriloChris picked up the remote, gave Paul a knowing nod and smiled. THIS was his moment.

He composed himself, took a deep breath and then ... threw the remote control at Jasper.

He completely missed.

'WHAT ARE YOU DOING?' said Paul, not that VentriloChris could understand a word. Jasper was almost out the door.

Crazy Red-Eye Paul was now back up on his feet and leaning against the toy helicopter. 'I guess it's up to me,' he said, and he kicked the remote control over to Dylan instead. 'You know what to do ...'

Dylan picked up the remote control, and instead of throwing it (which was an utterly STUPID thing to do), he shot the helicopter into the air, Red-Eye hanging from the bottom by his tail. He plummeted the chopper into a dive aimed directly at Jasper who had just made it to the exit. Being a showman, he decided to turn around and blow the superheroes a kiss …

'K'POOOOOOOOOOOWWWWWW!' screamed Red-Eye, his feet out in front of him. THUD. He landed a tiny drop kick directly to Jasper's face.

Then Red-Eye crashed to the floor head-first and was knocked out cold. But the helicopter smashed into Jasper sending him flying to the floor.

Iffi and Fifi seized the opportunity and both jumped on top of him at the same time.

'Did I get him?' said Red-Eye, as he slowly regained consciousness.

'Absolutely,' said Dylan, picking him up and resting him on his shoulder. 'His days of manipulating good-natured but vulnerable people are over.'

The policeman headed over to Jasper and handcuffed him.

'You know, I'm going to have to take you down to the station too, Repeat Offender,' said the policeman reluctantly.

'I know. I deserve to be punished,' said Zac.

'For what it's worth, I believe you too.' He turned to face the group of confused officers at the front door. 'Right, you lot, about time you turned up. One of you take this kid in, no need for handcuffs, he has given himself up willingly.'

'I will have to take that cat from you

I'm afraid,' said another of the policemen, moving to pick up the cat. He was met by a vicious hiss and narrowly avoided a savage swipe of the cat's claws. 'Or you could keep him. That's cool too.'

Jasper was dragged out by the policeman, who tipped his hat at Dylan and his team as he walked past. Zac stopped momentarily when he reached them. He bowed his head and looked as though he was about to apologise again.

'CUPCAKE!' shouted a girl entering the bank. Dylan looked over to see a cool girl with long brown hair, and a pair of pink sunglasses balanced on top of her head. 'You found Cupcake, oh, thank you, thank you,

THANK YOU!'

The cool girl ran over to Zac and picked up Cupcake who snuggled deep into her shoulder, not a claw or fang in sight.

'Wait, Keith's name is actually Cupcake? SERIOUSLY?' said Paul, remembering the ordeal they had been through to get him into the cage at Pets Behaving Badly.

'Seems quite nice around her, and Repeat Offender, for that matter,' added Pauline.

'I saw Cupcake on the news, stuck up a tree and ran straight over. Thank you so much for saving him.' The cool girl looked up for the first time at the boy who had been holding Cupcake. 'Zac?' she said, lost for words, much like he had been the first time they had met.

'Uh ... I ... Uh ...' And the second time they had met.

'I can't believe it! I haven't seen you since ...'

'I'm ... sorry,' said Zac, once more bowing his head.

'For what? For saving Cupcake? You're my HERO!' she said and kissed him gently on the cheek. 'I'm Esmé by the way.'

Zac raised his head, his cheeks as red as a sun-blushed tomato dipped in ketchup. And, for the first time in a long time, he smiled.

'Right, that's enough. We really need to take you down to the station, Repeat Offender.'

'Repeat Offender?' said Esmé, taking a small step backwards. 'The supervillain?'

'It's been a pleasure working with you, Repeat Offender,' said Dylan, stepping in and offering his hand. 'I must say you are the best undercover superhero I have ever worked with. I will be reporting back to Ron Strongman with very high praise indeed.'

Zac shook his hand, a smile stretching from ear to ear.

'I always knew there was something good in you Zac,' said Esmé. Her cheeks were rose-red.

Zac nodded appreciatively at Dylan as he left the bank, side by side with Esmé.

Dylan gathered his team around him.

'I wanted to thank each and every one of you for your efforts today. You all did so well, I mean, where on earth did you get those remote-control vehicles?'

'We stole them from a couple of kids who were playing with them outside,' said Red-Eye.

'Yeah, we should really give them back,' added Pauline.

'Yes you should,' said Dylan unable to hold back a little chuckle. They really were a group of mischievous iguanas. 'As I was saying, you all played a massive part in bringing down a *master criminal* today,' said Dylan.

'Don't do yourself down on your

first major victory, Iguana Boy,' said VentriloChris. 'Like many great superheroes before us, we brought down a real-life SUPERVILLAIN!'

'I don't see it that way. I think we took down a master criminal, who had *manipulated* a young and rather promising potential superhero. If that means we don't get credited as taking down a real-life supervillain, then so be it.'

'I'm with you, Dylan, he genuinely seemed really sorry for his actions,' said Iffi, putting her hand out in front of her.

'Yeah, we will take down a supervillain eventually, only a matter of time,' said VentriloChris, his hand joining the group.

'WHAT FOOL WOULD MESS WITH US?' shouted Terrifying Suzanne, her hand thundering down on top of VentriloChris'.

Next to put their hand in was Pauline, followed by Red-Eye, Smelly Paul and Paul. Finally, Dylan put his hand into the circle.

'To the CITD,' he said.

They all raised their hands and cheered.

'To the CITD.'

'To POOP!' screamed VentriloChris.

EPILOGUE

'Ah, Iguana Boy, good to see you. Please, take a seat,' said Ron, standing behind his desk and pointing towards an empty chair.

'You wanted to see me, sir?' said Dylan, sitting down.

'Yes, I did, I wanted to be the first to let you know that you have won our September Superstar award!'

'Are you sure? I didn't capture a supervillain, and besides, even if I had, it was a team effort.'

'Yes, yes of course it was a team effort,

but a team effort would be nothing without strong leadership, and you showed every sign of that.'

'Thank you, Mr Strongman.'

'And what of the newest addition to your team. How's he doing?'

'He's doing great. Getting along with everyone and eternally grateful at being given the opportunity to prove he is a good person.'

It had taken some convincing, but Dylan was determined not to let Repeat Offender waste his potential behind bars. He had managed to persuade the police that it was all one big undercover opportunity to capture a master criminal. Ron Strongman hadn't believed a word of it, of course, but he had trusted Dylan to keep an eye on Zac under Ron Strongman's leadership.

We have changed the name from Superstar, you know, to fit in with the rebranding. Congratulations, you are our first ever—'

'POOPERstar. I'm speechless,' said Dylan. He really was. The worst part was he still felt enormously proud (although he would put a hold on the business cards he was going to order).

'I would say that POOP is coming up smelling of roses right now.' said Ron Strongman. 'I'm sure there is something a little more *worthwhile* we could have you and that team of yours doing.'

'Not at all, Mr Strongman,' said Dylan, taking Ron, and himself by surprise. 'We provide a valuable service. We show people that we aren't only here to protect them, but that we care. And I am proud to be the person in charge of that here at ... POOP.' He still struggled to say the name, it was just so ridiculous. 'And I couldn't ask for a better team, so if it's all the same to you, we would like to continue our work.

'Of course, should we be called out to save a cat from a tree and another crime was happening in the vicinity of that tree, and we just so happened to witness it ...'

'You couldn't stand idly by,' said Ron Strongman with a knowing smile.

RON STRONGMAN
C.E.O.
POOPER
STAR
IGUANA BOY
I.B.

MEET THE CITD

SUPERHERO COLLECTIVE HQ ID PASS

NAME: DYLAN SPENCER

AKA: IGUANA BOY

SUPERPOWER: TALKING TO IGUANAS

AGE/HEIGHT: 9yrs/4ft 3ins

DISGUISE: CAPE!

FAVOURITE ANIMAL: IGUANAS

FAVOURITE PIZZA TOPPING: TRIPLE CHEESE

SUPERHERO COLLECTIVE HQ ID PASS

NAME: CHRIS

AKA: VENTRILOCHRIS

SUPERPOWER: VOICE THROWING

AGE/HEIGHT: 10yrs/3ft 2ins

DISGUISE: SNAZZY JUMPSUIT

FAVOURITE HOBBY: WHISPERING TO PEOPLE 20 METRES AWAY

SUPERHERO COLLECTIVE HQ ID PASS

NAME: SUZANNE

AKA: TERRIFYING SUZANNE

SUPERPOWER:
BEING TERRIFYING

AGE/HEIGHT: 7yrs/3ft 5ins

DISGUISE: N/A

FAVOURITE HOBBY: SHOUTING

P.O.O.P.

P.O.O.P.

HAVE YOU READ THE STORY OF IGUANA BOY SAVING THE WORLD WITH A TRIPLE CHEESE PIZZA?

P.O.O.P.